PAPER BOATS & BUTTERFLIES

True Tears

Sue Upton

Illustrations by Becky Stewart

Sue Upton
info@sueupton-author.com
First Published: June 2020
by
Budding Authors Assistant
www.help2publish.co.uk
Illustrations by Becky Stewart
Cover design by Lauren Zorkoczy

ISBN:- 9798650870326

To Nathan, Abigail and Jake

Chapter 1

The pain was excruciating. Sweat dripped from her forehead, and her face twisted as the agony continued. Hot air blasted pale skin, and ice-cold water poured down into her mouth. Miranda, spluttering and spitting, turned to one side and struck something hard. Pushing against it with both hands, she realised she was trapped. Moaning, she thrashed her arms and legs, until screams broke the air.

A dark shadow stood before her. She blinked and then shut her eyes again.

"No... no... please don't!"

"Miranda." The voice was gentle. "You're safe."

"Get away from me! I am not Miranda; I am Z89 Marcon."

"Miranda, sweetheart, it's me, Patrick. Your father. Don't be scared. You're having a bad dream."

"You're lying. I don't have a father!"

Silence.

A light glimmered through her tight eyelids.

Another voice. "What's wrong with her?"

"Another nightmare."

Miranda struggled out of the faraway world she was inhabiting and wiping sleep from her grey eyes she returned to the present. Patrick was kneeling on the rug and Stella was standing near the floor-length curtains, biting her nails.

Rubbing her eyes hard, Miranda focused on the face of her father. Patrick stretched his arms out towards her, but she pulled herself away to a sitting position, wrapping her arms around her knees.

"I'm sorry. It won't happen again," Miranda whispered.

"Everything is all right, lovely girl. This isn't your fault." Patrick rocked back on his heels and stood, his knees complaining with pops and cracks. "Come on, let's get you back into bed. You can't sleep on the floor."

Miranda looked around her. That night she had made a nest of pillows and the duvet between the wall and the enormous bed. She felt more comfortable in this enclosed space. This space was the same size as her Nod Pod in Zephyr, her place of safety.

Looking across at the two strangers – her parents – she crawled onto the bed beside her, pulling the duvet with her. She had removed the cover and pillowcases, so everything was white. The blue and gold patterned cover and cases lay folded neatly on the floor.

"Shall I make your bed for you, darling?" Stella said, picking up the pile.

Shaking her head, her eyes wide, Miranda stared at her, clutching the duvet. "White, white, white!" she stammered.

Patrick nodded and taking Stella's arm, he steered her towards the door. "Try and sleep," he said, turning off the light and pulling the door closed.

Miranda Winslow (Z89 Marcon) closed her eyes and slept.

The pain was excruciating. Sweat dripped from her forehead, and her face twisted as the agony continued. Hot air blasted pale skin, and ice-cold water poured down into her mouth. Z84, spluttering, and spitting, turned to one side and struck something hard. Pushing against it with both hands, she realised she was trapped. Moaning, she thrashed her arms and legs, until screams broke the air.

A dark shadow stood before her. She blinked and then shut her eyes again.

"No... no... please don't!"

"Z84." The voice was harsh. "You're vulnerable."

"Get away from me! I am not Z84; I am Erin Winslow."

"Z84 Marcon, it's me, Esme Dorling. Your school principal. You are scared. You are not having a bad dream; this is reality."

"You're lying!"

Silence.

A light glimmered through her tight eyelids.

4

Another voice. "Shall I stop, Miss Dorling?"

"Yes, for now."

Z84 struggled out of the pit, wiping tears from her grey eyes and knelt on the cold, stone floor. A figure in purple was standing looking down at her while another person, dressed in brown, leaned against a computer desk.

Rubbing her eyes hard, Z84 focused on the face of the school principal. Miss Dorling was stretching towards her, purple talons ready to scratch and scrape at her bare skin. Z84 pulled herself away to a sitting position, wrapping her arms around her knees.

"I'm sorry. It won't happen again," Z84 whispered.

"No, it won't; this is your own fault." Miss Dorling turned on her high, purple heels and clicked away.

"Come on, get back to your Nod Pod. You can't sleep here!" the Orderly barked.

Once there, Z84 looked around her. She felt so uncomfortable in this enclosed space. This was not her place of safety. Everything was white. She craved colour and pattern and pictures. Shaking her head, her eyes wide, Z84 crawled onto her bed, clutching a sheet. "White, white, white!" she stammered.

The light was extinguished, and the window of the Pod was shut.

Z84 Marcon (Erin Winslow) closed her eyes and slept.

Report: 2462

To: John Johnson, Joyce Williams, Oliver Irons

From: Esme Dorling

Z89 behaviour as expected.

- No attachment to parents

- Achievement at school – exceptional in science

- Desires the regimented structure and disciplinary regime of Zephyr

Z84 behaviour as expected.

- Misses her family

- Achievement – exceptional in art

- Desires the relaxed structure and defective regime of the outside world

Please reply with next action.

Chapter 2

Miranda closed her history book and handed it to the teacher. She still couldn't believe so many books were available for her to read; they weren't under lock and key. Reading and writing were encouraged; giving your opinion was accepted; making friends was expected.

The sudden chatter around her marked the end of the lesson; a raucous bell summoned them to the next one. On leaving the classroom, her new friend Petra caught up with her.

"I hate history, don't you?"

"I like it," Miranda replied in a soft voice. Then with more confidence, she added, "I find it very interesting. People in this country once fought against each other and killed a king."

"A good idea too and good riddance to the monarchy." A deep voice came from behind as they climbed the stairs to the first floor and science.

Reaching the top of the stairs and turning abruptly, Petra threw a comment back. "Trust you to say that, Rob."

The boy grinned. He raised his hands, nails daubed in black varnish, entreating them to see his point of view. "How do they help you? They cost the country millions!" Miranda could see he was warming to an impassioned speech. "Good money that could be spent on better education and hospitals." He waved his arms dramatically. "All men are born equal," he added as they lined up outside the physics lab.

The science teacher was waiting for quiet, but Petra had to have the final word. "Communist pig!"

"What was that, Petra Truman?" Dr Boatman made his way down the line towards them. "Would you like to discuss my politics at break time? It can all be arranged." His voice was brittle.

Petra went decidedly pink and swallowed. "Not you, sir. Sorry, sir. I was talking to him." She pointed to the boy beside her.

"Ah, Mr Lombardi." Dr Boatman's gaze now fell on Roberto's attire. "Since when have leather jackets become school uniform, pray tell?"

Rob scratched his head. "Come the revolution, sir, anything will be allowed!"

"That's as maybe, but apart from the fact that you're not revolting just yet, let's get rid of it, shall we?"

"Yes, sir." The white-haired, yet sprightly teacher strode back to the door; Rob stood to attention and performed a pretend salute towards his retreating back.

"Right then class, in we go. A little bit of friction out here and lots of learning about the same force awaits you in there." His hazel eyes twinkled under snowy eyebrows.

When Miranda reached the open door, the teacher smiled benevolently at her. "Ah, the twin who came home. Lovely to see you, my dear. You're so much better at science than your sister. I do hope Erin is settled into her new boarding school and not getting into too much trouble. She was often in detention." Dr Boatman frowned. "I think your parents were right to move her."

In answer, Miranda just nodded, not wanting to discuss her sister, and followed the other students into the laboratory. She was mystified with the teacher's decision to not punish Petra and Rob. In her previous school, Zephyr, there would have been severe recriminations. Once she had settled on one of the spindly stools, she thought about her life and education up until just a few months ago; it had all changed in such a short time. This caused an image of her twin sister, Erin, to flash before her eyes. Guilt at leaving Erin in the Zephyr school in Cornwall washed over her, and she gasped.

Z84, exhausted from being subjected to more punishments, or experiments, as the teachers liked to call them – each one testing her mind as well as her physical strength – struggled into wakefulness.

A sharp click from the wall opposite her bed indicated the opening of the daily uniform drawer. Dragging herself out of bed and holding her breath, she peeped inside the compartment. Please don't let it be grey, she inwardly prayed. White clothing was nestled inside. Oh, thank goodness – a normal day – she thought, expelling the pent-up air with a sigh.

After showering, the petite girl dressed quickly. Z84 rubbed her hand through her stubby hair and wished there was a mirror to check her face. She missed having her make-up and hair stuff. She missed having hair! She missed... and at this thought, she broke down. Z84, or Erin as she used to be known, missed her family, friends, freedom, and even her school. Her heart had been ripped out when her family left her behind.

I will never get used to this new life, she thought. The last few, slow months, since being smuggled into this dreadful underground school in a coffin, have been the longest I've ever experienced. Each day an eternity, especially the gruesome, grey uniform days. How many tears will fall before I can get out of here?

They had just been trying to find their sister, Miranda. Her brother, Malachi, along with his girlfriend, Cara Mallory, had helped Z84, Erin, to gain access to the school which lay beneath Bodmin Moor in Cornwall. Once an old, decommissioned nuclear bunker, it was now transformed into a school called Zephyr and held 120 students, all of whom had been born in 2000. Each student's twin lived somewhere in Britain. Miss Dorling, the school principal, explained all of this to Z84 on her induction to Zephyr. According to her, Britain was no longer producing the right workforce. The British government, through Trefoil, had invested a great deal of money in establishing the school for a trial period.

Wiping her eyes, Z84 thought about the day ahead. Learning was the priority on a white uniform day, the colour of purity. Surprising herself, she looked forward to these days – a complete contrast to her school days in Newton, her hometown, a million miles away from this place. There she hated school, only enjoying her art where she could lose herself in the creation and construction process. Here, art was only offered on the blue uniform days; she hadn't experienced many so far. Perhaps, she thought, if I work hard today and follow their draconian rules, I could have an art day.

A loud ringing filled her tiny Nod Pod, ordering her to breakfast, and the glass window in the end wall slid open. Z84 climbed down the ladder outside and joined the other students, some in white, some in grey, and some in blue. The line of girls snaked along the corridor to the Nourishment Sector. Once there, the line of boys joined them, their Nod Pods being on the opposite side of the school.

No one spoke.

Soft music accompanied them while they collected their breakfast of bacon, eggs and toast; there was no choice. They were fed well here most of the time. Food nourishes the mind and body, as Miss Dorling reminded them. Like servile robots, they placed their trays on the tables in their designated area and remained standing.

Z84 looked across the table and caught the eye of one of the boys. He winked at her, and she tried not to smile, clamping her lips together and taking on a serious face. Z42 then moved his forefinger to touch his thumb, creating a teardrop shape. Only a tiny gesture, but one that Z84 recognised as she had seen it many times since her arrival at Zephyr. She returned the gesture without looking at him; a connection made.

A monotone voice filled the room. "You are one being. You belong here. You are loved."

"We are one being. We belong here. We are loved." The students repeated the morning phrase three times and then sat down to eat.

Later, in one of the Learning Labs, Z84 faced a computer screen. The room could hold about 20 students, so both Marcon and Febcon were installed in there studying. Each contingent was made up of 10 students, five boys and five girls, all born on the first of the month: Marcon being the contingent born on 1st March, Febcon on 1st February.

This Learning Lab was a large light room with state-of-the-art computer systems, not dissimilar to the IT rooms in Z84's school back in Newton, but here, there were far more restrictions on the information you could access. She wished she had paid more attention at her previous school so she would know how to bypass the systems to access YouTube and Instagram.

Her thoughts were suddenly broken by the teacher barking out instructions.

"Put on your headphones! You should hear my voice through these. Raise your hand if you have a problem." No one dared. The teacher continued.

"You will see on the screen, charts and data for 2015, on how the present government runs the United Kingdom." Z84 studied her screen carefully and made out various figures that corresponded to different departments – education, housing, defence, medical care.

"Answer the questions that will flash onto your screen. I will now communicate with you individually through your headphones to guide you, when necessary."

Z84 had never been interested in politics, but having experienced grey days, and desperate for a blue one, she focused all her attention on the work.

She was astonished to find it interesting, and the time flew by.

The lesson finished with the teacher asking them to save their work and then telling them to file out in silence. As Z84 joined the others, she caught sight of Z63, a very pretty girl who smiled for a second before looking down at the floor. Z84 still couldn't believe this girl was Petra's twin.

Walking to the next sector allowed her time to reflect on how she came to be in Zephyr.

Suspecting her parents of having secrets, she had persuaded her brother, Mal, to follow them to Cornwall. On arriving at a hotel, she entered a dining room full of people, each table occupied by two adults and one teenager. It was 1st March, her birthday, and Z84, then known as Erin, discovered her parents with a young girl – her identical twin sister, Miranda, and Z63 was seated at a table with Petra's parents. The girl, a carbon copy of Petra, ignored her. Then, assuming the girl was her best friend, Z84 grew angry. Now she knew the truth.

She had known Petra since infant school, and they became close. Like any relationship, regardless of the many ups and downs, they were always there for each other until the subject of being a twin was introduced. How silly we were. Petra doesn't believe she has a twin! What would she make of all this? This place where children are tormented and degraded.

Just to make it all worse, Petra had gone behind her back, meeting up with Shay, a boy Z84 had liked for a long time. She had observed them together and could see, from their actions and words, they were now a couple.

Z84 came out of her musing for a moment. None of this mattered now; it was in the distant past. Now, it was about staying alive. Ahead of her in the line was Z42, someone who was helping her to do just that, someone she could finally trust.

She had only been installed in Zephyr for a short time when she discovered Z42 was planning to escape. He and some of the other students were gaining skills and knowledge and starting to use them to their advantage and not to that of Trefoil; the organisation who were the decision-makers behind Zephyr. With her experience of the outside world, she had changed their ideas drastically.

Z42 contacted her firstly via a computer screen, having managed to override the system to communicate with other students, and then through the Illusion/Delusion (ID) equipment used in the Orientation Sector, where he had bypassed the program.

Sitting in the Learning Lab, precisely one week after entering Zephyr, she had been studying quadratic equations. An image of tears began falling down the screen until her work was hidden. Z84 had been scared at first because she didn't know what it meant. Tentatively looking around her, she had seen first one, then another student, touch their thumb to their forefinger, the other three fingers enclosing the tear shape. Some held the gesture as they pretended to scratch their head, others just lowered their arm and made the slight movement, a hardly noticeable sign which the Teardrops used to communicate; it brought them all together. Z84 looked again at the screen. A message was now forming amongst the falling tears.

"We have shed many tears. Will you help and become one of us?"

Not knowing how to respond and thinking it was a trap, the girl didn't do anything at first.

"We know you are Z89's twin. We know you have come from the outside. You have the knowledge that can help us escape. We are the Teardrops." Then below this, "Z42."

The line of students arrived at their next destination, the Orientation Sector and Z84 brought her mind back to the present. They filed into the room. Each wall was sectioned off, and each student entered an alcove. Z84 made her way across the room and stepped onto the treadmill sitting within the enclosed area. The ID headset swung into place, and in an instant, she found herself in a grassy park with colourful flower beds and trees of every kind of green. The warmth of the sun comforted her bones, and for a moment or two, she could pretend she was back in the outside world.

Around her were other students, all standing, waiting for instructions.

A voice came loud and clear. "You may start walking now."

The treadmills began to power up, and Z84 started to walk towards a path meandering through the trees. She was joined by Z42. He always hunched over to try and make himself less conspicuous, but he stood out head and shoulders, literally, above the rest. He made the teardrop shape with his fingers, and she returned the gesture. As their fingers touched, a gentle warmth flowed through Z84, and she relaxed.

"You may talk." The voice broke into her reverie, and gradually a gentle hum of young people talking and laughing began to flow softly through the trees.

"What have you found out?" Z42 asked.

"$E=MC^2$."

She knew they were watching their every move. They had nearly been caught communicating this way before, resulting in Z42 hacking into the ID program and ensuring the teachers couldn't follow any discourse, but they still remained vigilant.

E was Edward – an Orderly working in the school and was their only contact with the outside world. He, along with Pandora, a funeral director from nearby Castleton, had helped smuggle her into Zephyr to find Miranda. M was her 18-year-old brother Malachi. C was Cara, Mal's girlfriend, who had some sort of link with the school and whom Z84 didn't trust. Cara lived in Castleton with her father, Professor Mallory, and she was responsible for Z84 being incarcerated inside Zephyr, a secret school lying beneath the ground. The squared meant that everything was in place. They were going to get them out.

They were surrounded by green trees and rose bushes, and, as they continued walking, a lake reflecting the azure blue of the sky above opened out in front of them. She knew though; this was an illusion, that it was the ID equipment attached to her head that was making her mind think they were in beautiful parkland and it was the treadmill below her feet making her walk. The fresh air being pumped into the room and the heat lamps on the ceiling were creating a sunny July day.

"That's good." Z42 looked pleased. He rubbed his hand over his stubby head, the red hair beginning to sprout. Just like him, his hair never gave up fighting; however much they shaved his head. All the students had their hair shaved – to remove their identity, to make them all the same, yet Z84 could see each boy and girl there were unique in appearance and in their skills.

"When?" Z42 asked. They were winding their way through the woods following the path. Ahead of them, two students, a boy and a girl waited for them.

"1-9-15. The day they reach their five-year phase and leave Zephyr to meet their parents for lunch."

"That will be Sepcon, not us."

"Yes. E will swap two of the September contingent for us."

"Just two? Why?"

Z84 stopped suddenly. "We can do more outside than in."

"That makes sense." Z42 looked at her then and smiled. "We must talk to the others."

"Yes, I want to talk to Z63." She gestured towards the girl, who was an exact copy of her best friend, Petra, standing beside the lake. Z84 Marcon made the teardrop sign, and Z42 Febcon followed suit, touching her hand briefly. Their fingers were a butterfly shape for a second, and then the wings were torn apart as they went their separate ways.

Report: 2463

To: Esme Dorling

From: John Johnson, Joyce Williams, Oliver Irons

You seem to have turned around your previous disaster of the twins – Z84 and Z89 – discovering each other. This will be used to our advantage.

1) Correction penalties will be put in place for Winslow. However, with Stella Winslow's assistance, the transition has been smooth.

2) Recompense to go to Cara Mallory for her service to Trefoil.

Next steps – close monitoring MUST continue. Remember, Esme, you can be terminated at any time. We have many others ready to take your place.

Chapter 3

Miranda stared out of the floor to ceiling window in her room knowing her sister, Erin, would have done the same. Across the road and nestled in the long grass in the field opposite, sat the Seven Spirits – seven large stones sitting in a circle forever waiting to be woken from their enforced sleep. Seven people who danced there once were transformed, according to an ancient legend, into solid rock due to breaking the laws of the Sabbath.

Now, it was 2015. A hot July day and the whole weekend ahead. The summer break wasn't far away; in fact, in just a few days, they were free to enjoy six weeks away from school. Miranda was not looking forward to it. She liked to learn, she needed routine and she wasn't very good at finding things to do. Having been held in a school where long periods of free time didn't exist, she felt apprehensive about the coming weeks. Petra and the others had said they would be around to keep her occupied, but some of them were going away on holiday, whatever that was!

Going across to the shelves lining one wall, Miranda scanned the rows of books: historical fiction, graphic novels, revision textbooks, science fiction, dystopian stories, and so many other genres she had never seen before. She breathed in the dry, woody smell of the pages, savouring the pleasure of touching the glossy spines, her heart racing at the thought of all these adventures she could dive into and not having to have these books all locked away.

On another shelf, some of Erin's sketchbooks were piled haphazardly. A small wooden jointed figure stood watching her – its legs and arms positioned as though it was running. Flicking through the oversized, rectangular pages of one of the books, she found drawings of people walking, crouching, sitting. There were unfinished sketches, close-ups of joints and muscles and then on the next few pages, there were fully completed images in different media; pastels, acrylics and soft pencil smudged to create shadow and depth.

My sister is a very talented artist. Zephyr despises art – I wonder what they will make of her talent? She traced her finger over the outlines just as Erin would have laid her pencil or brush onto the paper. I wish I could do this. If only life had been different, I might have become an artist too. Perhaps as her twin, I also have these skills. Lost in her memories, Miranda wasn't fully aware of a soft knock on the door, but then a series of louder knocks brought her back to the present.

"Hello."

"Hi. Can I come in?" It was Mal, her older brother.

"Yes, of course." Closing the art book and placing it back on the shelf, pushing the other books into a neat pile, she waited for him to enter the room and to settle on the sofa. The room was huge compared to her Nod Pod in Zephyr; enough space for a double bed, a sofa and armchair, a large television set, a long desk and swivel chair and a large airy bathroom that was hidden behind a door in one of the walls.

"We have some news from Edward."

"Good news, I hope." Miranda perched herself on the edge of the armchair and looked across at the deeply tanned young man before her. He was wearing shorts and a bright red T-shirt; his feet were bare. Miranda was still shy when she was with him or Stella and Patrick, her parents; she wasn't used to having a family. They were all so kind, she was beginning to trust them and realised they really cared about her.

"He says we can get them out on 1st September when the September Contingent go out to meet their parents. He's arranged to swap Erin and a boy with two from the group. He'll help us to smuggle them out of the hotel."

"Will they be safe? They had armed guards when I was there for my five-year phase."

"We have to try something, and this sounds our best bet. This gives us just over a month to finalise arrangements. Cara says her father has also offered to help. We'll have to have somewhere they can hide. Cara's house is nice and close in Castleton, not far from

Zephyr, and that would give us time to think about our next move."

Miranda could see Mal was keen on this idea, but she was scared. What if it goes wrong? Biting her lip, and frowning, she rubbed her hand over her short black hair – it was slowly growing back, and she loved to touch it. It helped her believe this was all real, and she wasn't going to wake up in a cell from a dreadful nightmare.

"What about Stella and Patrick? Are we going to tell them?"

"You mean Mum and Dad." Mal grinned at her. "You need to start getting used to not calling them by their first names."

"I know. There's just so much to get used to. Sometimes it overwhelms me, and I don't know what to do. Sometimes I even wish I was back in Zephyr."

Mal looked at her, his brown eyes wide. "Why do you say that? From what I could see on my short visit, I wouldn't want to be there."

"Tell me what you saw, Mal." Miranda wanted to see it from his point of view.

"Well, we came into a farmhouse. Erin and I had visited it before totally unaware of what lay beneath it. Inside it was completely normal, a big kitchen with space for a table and chairs; a dog lying in front of the open fire; washing hanging on wooden rails that swung from the ceiling. We were escorted by a man who we had believed to be the farmer, towards a back room where a pair of wooden doors were opened revealing a set of metal doors to a lift: big enough to hold 12 people, or so the little plaque on the wall said."

Miranda sat forward. "Did the lift go down into an enormous area where there was a waterfall and lots of plants?" She remembered being taken to the Central Hub to see Miss Dorling.

"Yes, that's right," agreed Mal, nodding. "The lift walls were made of glass, so there was a good view of the area. It was octagonal in shape. Soaring white walls - three or four storeys high. We were met by three people, one dressed in purple. I'd seen her before..."

"That's Miss Dorling," interrupted Miranda.

"Yes, and there was a Mr Garnet dressed in a red suit and a thin woman dressed in beige. We weren't told her name."

"That's one of the Administrators. They have no name."

"Really?" Mal was confused. "How come?"

Miranda explained, "They have no names just A1, A2 and so on or O1, O2. The Administrators wear beige, and the Orderlies are in brown."

"What is with all the different colours?" Mal asked. "The teachers all looked like bright peacocks against the drab colours of the students and the other staff. Is it like a hierarchy? I remember being told in history only the monarchy could wear purple in Elizabethan times; it wasn't a colour for the masses. Do you have to treat Miss Dorling like royalty?" This last question was accompanied by a wide grin, and Miranda reflected his expression.

"No, we don't have to bow to her," she laughed. "I think it could be about leadership, though," agreed Miranda. "I'm not entirely sure what it all means."

"What about you? Why were you called Z89 and not Miranda?"

"As you know, all of the students have a number, not a name. This corresponds to the time of their birth. I am Z89, so I was born at nine minutes past eight in the morning on 1ˢᵗ March 2000."

"So, that's why Erin is now known as Z84 Marcon. It's all down to their birthday."

"Yes, Erin is Z84." Miranda thought about the words Mal had used, and then asked, "What is a birthday? I remember Stella saying something about that when we met in the hotel."

Mal gaped at her. "You know - it's a special day – you're given presents and cake, and if you're really lucky you have a party. I had a brilliant party for my eighteenth last December. Mum and Dad gave me a car."

"A car! That's amazing. A sort of celebration, I suppose?"

"Yes, that's right. What did you do in Zephyr?"

"Nothing." Miranda folded her arms and pondered for a moment, gazing into space. "Is that why they allowed us out this year on 1ˢᵗ March. I remember doing that twice before, and each time Patrick gave me a paper boat with a hidden message. Stella always offered me something too, and the teachers would get rid of it."

Mal jumped to his feet. "The butterfly brooch! I'd forgotten all about that! It's still in my car. I'll fetch it!" Pulling open the door, he stopped in his tracks. Patrick was revealed with his hand raised ready to knock on the door.

"Hi, sorry to interrupt you guys, but dinner's ready."

Z84 was wearing dark blue. Finally, she had been rewarded for her efforts in lessons. She was shown into a room like the one where she had finally met her twin. This room was light and bright, with ocean walls and a soft sapphire carpet; an indigo coloured sofa, piled with sky-blue cushions; art materials on a cobalt acrylic desk and a squat kettle boiling away merrily in the corner. An Orderly, dressed in brown, stood with his back to her, clouds of steam wafting around him like a London fog. It smells like he's making coffee, she thought to herself, and found her mouth was watering - she hadn't drunk coffee for such a long time. He turned towards her - it was Edward.

"Good morning, Z84," he said, bringing over a steaming mug of coffee and a piece of chocolate cake and placing them on a table beside her. "How are you?"

"I'm good, thank you. How are you?" She looked at his very upright figure, noting his haggard face.

"I am as well as can be expected."

"Is it safe?" Z84 whispered.

In answer, he nodded towards the cake which sat on top of a paper napkin. "I will be just outside if you need anything."

"Thank you." Once she was alone, she sipped her coffee and scooped up some gooey fudge icing with a fork. She closed her eyes luxuriating in the flavours bombarding her tongue, the heady aromas swirling through the air. Opening her eyes to look at where to place her fork for the next chocolatey mouthful, she saw what looked like words on the paper below. Scraping away the cake, and stuffing it into her mouth, a message began to take shape. It was smudged in places, and once the cake had all been consumed, she could make out the message which read:

Tomorrow you will be abusive towards a teacher, and so the next day you will be given grey to wear. I am on duty in the Correction Sector then.

Z84 wiped her mouth with the napkin, obliterating some of the words. Then just to be sure, she knocked back the coffee and clumsily dropping the mug onto the desk, she spilt the last few dregs. In case anyone was observing her, she uttered, "Ooh, butterfingers!" and mopped it up with the napkin. It was now a sodden pulp and safe to put into the bin.

The next few hours flew by as Z84 drew and painted images from her past life: Fizz and Pop, two pet Labradors owned by her grandparents; the Seven Spirits, the stones near the house and finally a picture of her mother. This last one was a pencil sketch and showed Stella in a floor-length black dress with strings of pearls entwining her long neck, and a fake white fur stole wrapped around bony shoulders. She remembered her parents going to a charity ball a whole lifetime ago, her father in a white tuxedo and black bow tie, her mother looking young and carefree. Both happy and contented. At the time, Z84 had never suspected they were keeping secrets from her. She studied the final drawing of her mother with a critical eye. Without thinking, she had sketched Stella's face as mournful and desolate; the whole image saturated with sorrow.

A sharp pain bore into her chest: the agony of loss and rejection. Z84 stroked the paper desperate to see her mother again, hoping this would make her materialise before her, knowing that magic like that didn't exist. "I love you, Mum," she whispered. Yet you were so cruel to leave me here. You could be strict at times, and we argued over stupid stuff like makeup and homework, typical mother-daughter arguments, but this time it was different; surely, you haven't abandoned me. Another voice inside her head interrupted her – she abandoned your sister; she can do the same to you. Miss Dorling's words echoed once again, "They don't need you anymore."

She shook her head; none of this made any sense. I know she loves me. Perhaps Mum was forced to behave the way she did. Perhaps she was being threatened. In her mind's eye, she recalled how Stella had reacted to her and Mal appearing at their hotel in Cornwall. Mum was terrified, what if they find out? The 'they' must be Trefoil. Once I am out of this prison, I want answers. This thought made her more determined to escape. Tidying up the pencils and paper, she thought about what they needed to do. What could she do tomorrow to ensure she saw Edward the following day? A fledgling of a plan formed in her mind.

"How are you getting on?" A syrupy voice interrupted her thoughts, and she whirled round to be confronted by the sharp figure of Miss Dorling, a vision in violet.

Fighting to hide her true feelings about this woman, Z84 dropped the sketchbook she had been holding. Could the woman read minds? She wondered.

"Oh! Miss Dorling. Yes, I'm well, thank you," Z84 answered.

Miss Dorling leaned down, lifting the fallen book to her eye level. "Ah, a nice drawing of your mother."

"Thank you." Emotions now under control, Z84 picked up some scattered brushes and returned them to a pot on the desk.

"You're quite an artist, aren't you. That will come in useful one day." Esme Dorling glided across to the sofa and sat down, hooking her ankles tightly together, holding her body erect like a column of steel. She gestured to Z84 to also sit down, patting the space next to her.

Z84 chose to rest on the chair at the desk. She waited while Miss Dorling flicked through the pages.

"Your sister doesn't have your ability, but she was very good at making boats out of paper." She looked up from the book; the smile she gave was false, the look she gave was evil.

Z84 feigned surprise. "Really? I didn't know that."

"Yes, not much good for the future. A complete waste of time and effort, though she was very good at chemistry. Just like your grandfather."

Grandpops had been an engineer, Z84 said to herself.

"Silas Winslow won awards for chemistry," Miss Dorling continued.

"You're talking of Grandad, my dad's dad. I never really knew him. He and my grandmother were killed while skiing in the Alps. An avalanche, I think. I was only four when it happened."

"A dreadful shame. I hear he could have won the Nobel prize." Miss Dorling sneered, curling her lip. "So, your sister, Miranda, might be a great chemist too, one day."

Suddenly, Z84 leaned forward, clasping her hands together. "Why did you swap Miranda and me?"

Silence.

"I need to know."

The woman looked at her with narrowed eyes. "You don't need to know anything." She laid the sketchbook down beside her and folded her arms, forming a barrier between them. Tilting her angular face to one side, she seemed to be goading the young girl into speaking further.

Z84 wasn't going to be pushed. She waited. Two can play at this game, she thought. Sitting back against the cushioned back of the chair, she slowly folded her arms, mirroring Miss Dorling's posture.

Silence.

"Perhaps you are the more intelligent twin after all. We shall have to step up our investigations further.

You are an interesting specimen." Miss Dorling stood, straightening her statuesque body to its full height. She nodded, thus ending the conversation and strode towards the door. Z84 called out to her.

"I am not a specimen to be investigated. I am a human being, with feelings and dreams and desires."

Miss Dorling turned abruptly on her dagger heels. A smirk came to the woman's face. "You have been part of an experiment from the day you were born. You want to know why you are now here and why your sister is out there?" She gestured with a flick of her hands towards the door like a magician revealing a rabbit from a hat. "It is your own fault, poking your nose into things that don't concern you; disrupting our schedule; wanting to find your twin." A harsh laugh erupting from the woman startled the girl.

"We have decided you could be very useful to us in the future. It is you, not the other one who shows real spirit; it is you who interests us. We helped you along the way, of course, but it was your determination that got you here." While she was speaking, the door slid open, and she started toward the exit. Z84 was too quick for her though, darting past and now blocking the entrance. Miss Dorling stopped still and gaped.

"Get out of my way!" she shrieked.

"Why are you doing this? Why are you experimenting on children? This is what the Nazis did in the Second World War. What you're doing is barbaric!" Z84 shouted.

The hard slap knocked Z84 sideways. Shaking her head to recover, she suddenly felt sharp nails in her upper arms and warm breath on her face.

"Don't ever speak to me like that again!"

Spittle dripped down the girl's face. She tried to pull away, trying to think of karate moves that could help her escape, but this tall, sinewy woman held her tight, the nails digging in, cutting her skin. Abruptly, she let go, and Z84 found herself falling to the floor. The door slid back into place, and Z84 was left alone trembling, tears threatening to appear.

Breathing deeply, the girl rubbed her sore arms and made a promise to herself; she would do everything she could to find out what was going on here in this school and to escape.

Report: 2464

To: Esme Dorling

From: John Johnson, Joyce Williams, Oliver Irons

Metamorphosis Phase

Thought Reform must begin immediately, one contingent at a time.

Ensure this is programmed correctly to have full pliability of students.

Each student's gift must be protected.

Full details of programme – see attachment.

Chapter 4

When Mal first suggested watching some movies, Miranda was nervous and confused. She asked for paper and a pencil so she could make copious notes of the subject she was going to observe. At this, Mal shook his head, gestured for her to sit and proceeded to explain this was for relaxation.

"What is relaxation?" she asked.

"Well, it's when you take a break away from your work and studies. You chill out."

"Why would I want to do that? I don't like being cold."

Mal laughed. "Because your brain needs to have a rest sometime. We're now into the school holidays, and kids and teachers can have a rest. I need a rest after those exams. A-levels are such a drag!" He brought up several images on his TV, of films he thought Miranda might like before continuing.

"Chilling isn't about being cold; it's sort of letting go." Mal frowned. "How did you relax in your school?"

"We didn't. We exercised every day, which was nice. I suppose that was a rest from our studies."

Miranda's voice softened as she thought of the boy she had left behind, of the times they met and talked in the Orientation Sector. "We could speak to people too, but only for a short time."

Intrigued by the images appearing before her, Miranda pulled the leather beanbag close to the screen and made herself comfortable. It was a hot summer day, and yet she wasn't wearing the grey shorts Stella had bought for her. The bruising and blisters, from the final onslaught of punishment in Zephyr, when she had been subjected to immense heat and cold, extremes of sound and light, were finally healing. Miranda never wanted to wear grey clothes ever again. Now, delighting in wearing blue jeans and a blue T-shirt, she asked, "What is a 'toy' story?"

"Toys! You know about toys, right?"

"I know what a story is, but I'm not sure about toys. Are they scary?" Miranda gazed up at Mal.

"You play with toys when you're a child." Mal pressed the button on the remote control. "Look, I'll show you the movie, and you can see. I used to have toys like this when I was little. You might recognise some of the things you played with."

Miranda wasn't so sure; her childhood hadn't been good.

She soon became enthralled by the antics of Woody and giggled when Buzz tried to fly - emotions she had rarely experienced in Zephyr, where they were only shown educational documentaries. Miranda was entranced until a repeated pinging suddenly broke her concentration and glancing across at Mal, she saw him scanning his phone screen. He paused Buzz Lightyear in mid-flight.

"Miranda, you need to see this. It's from Cara," he said, passing his phone across to his sister. "What is Thought Reform?" His voice wavered.

Change of plan.

Edward said Thought Reform has begun.

Jancon completed. Febcon to begin 10th August.

Must bring them out 1st August, not wait until 1st September.

C xx

Miranda grew cold as she read the message. "That only gives us a few days to get organised," she said, looking across at her brother, his face tense, his hands held together in a tight ball.

Another ping and she passed the phone back to Mal. Reading aloud the words from the screen, Mal's speech wobbled. "Cara says, Thought Reform changes the belief patterns of a person." He looked up; all the colour drained from his face. "It sounds like brainwashing."

Miranda whispered, "This must be part of the next phase."

Mal chewed his lip and frowned. "What do you mean?"

"There are certain phases we go through as we grow up. I have been in Chrysalis Phase since turning ten. Before that, it was Embryonic, then Larval. Now I am fifteen I am entering Metamorphosis Phase."

"Like a butterfly?"

"Yes, I suppose so. Everyone must go through these phases before reaching maturity at 18."

"People don't go through those phases, Miranda, insects do. I don't know what's going on in that school, but this Thought Reform is serious stuff. Brainwashing isn't good," he announced. "Erin's in real danger! We must get her out of there." Mal staggered to his feet, punching his phone hard. "Cara? Hi, it's me. Can you talk?"

Cara's voice stormed into the room through the loudspeaker of Mal's phone. She sounded so close; Miranda looked to see if she had walked in.

"Yes. Our original plan can just be moved forwards to a different date. Augcon will be going out on 1st August. We'll just swap two of them with Erin and Z42 instead of Sepcon."

"Z42 is a Febcon. We need to move quickly!" urged Miranda, who was now on her feet. "Can we do it?"

A door crashing against a wall made Miranda spin round. "Can you do what?" Patrick shouted, his voice thick and unsteady. "Who are you talking to?" He entered the room stumbling over an array of trainers, clothes and books scattered around the floor, before tumbling headfirst onto the nearby sofa.

"Dad, are you okay?" Mal crossed the room to where his father lay, his limbs spread out like a starfish.

"I'm fine. Couldn't be better," he slurred into a cushion. A loud belch ended his sentence like a full stop, and a strong smell of alcohol permeated the room.

"I'll call you back," Mal said, switching off his phone. "Dad, you're drunk! Miranda, come and help me sit him up. I've never seen him like this."

Miranda hovered in the background. She stared at Patrick. "What's the matter with him? Is he ill?"

"I've been celebrating! You'll never guess what happened today." Patrick was now sitting, hunched over and struggling to find something in his pockets. "Eureka!" he exclaimed and held out his key ring waggling it in Mal's face. The Mercedes Smart key was missing. "Look no car! I lost it today when they gave me the push at work. I am now unemplooo, unammmm..." he tailed off and then tried again. "I don't have a job!" he shouted. "Me, no job," he added, slapping his hand against his chest. Then to their horror, his face contorted, tears oozed from bloodshot eyes, and he sobbed loudly into his hands.

"Come on, Dad, let's get you sorted out," he said as though speaking to a child. "Miranda, can you go and get Stella? She'll know what to do." She nodded and left the room.

Z84, along with the other nine Marcon students, watched Jancon enter the debating room. The five boys and five girls, all in white, selected their seats, and then everyone waited patiently for the teacher to begin.

Miss Citrine surveyed the room with a scowl. "Let's begin, shall we?" The question floated in the air. All the students, except one, knew it wasn't down to them to reply.

"Yes, let's," murmured Z84.

All eyes turned towards her, including Miss Citrine's. "Of course, Z84. I should have known you would have something to say," she growled. "Alright then, why don't you begin the debate? The question today is "Monarch or Parliament? Do we need both?""

Z84 thought for a moment. She was a bit out of her depth when it came to politics, but she did know her history. "Parliament has tried to get rid of the monarchy before, but to no avail. I think our queen is here to stay."

"Z11? What are your thoughts?" The teacher, dressed in a lemon trouser suit, turned her gaze to a boy from Jancon.

"I believe there is no necessity for a monarch or a parliament," he intoned. "Neither helps the common man or woman."

Z84 observed the boy. His face held no emotion, eyes blank, lips pressed in a taut line. His skull smooth and unblemished, no trace of hair showing. Wanting to understand his bland comment, she couldn't help herself and leaned forward, placing her elbows on her knees. "What do you mean?"

Miss Citrine nodded at Z11 to continue.

"They are all old people who don't understand how to improve our lives. The future of this world will be down to the young people."

The other nine Jancon students nodded their assent. Z11 resumed. "Our country is governed by various groups who do not fully represent the needs of the people."

"We can vote when we're eighteen w-w-when we leave Zephyr. We decide who will govern because we live in a democratic society." This was Z77's contribution to the debate. Miss Citrine glared at the boy whose face turned scarlet. "W-w-w-well, that's what we've been taught," he stuttered.

There was a moment of absolute quiet before the teacher bobbed her head at another student. Petra's twin, thought Z84, and threw a smile across to the girl sitting opposite her.

"I agree with Z77. Democracy is the best way," she said. "What's the alternative?"

41

"Z33 Jancon? What is your opinion?" Miss Citrine posed the question to a girl who was sitting just like Z11 with a very straight back, her face blank, her mouth drawn into a tight line.

"They are no use to us. We should kill them all!" she stated in a monotone.

Z84 couldn't believe what she was hearing or seeing as all the Jancon students stood up and clapped in unison at the girl's statement.

"Thank you, Jancon. You may sit down." Miss Citrine was smirking as she made notes. "A very interesting observation, Z33."

Z84 was shocked by Jancon's actions but more so by Miss Citrine's reaction; the teacher was pleased with their behaviour. How strange? She thought. The debate continued around her, some agreeing with Jancon and others very much against their views. The teacher agreed with some comments and then began to bring the lesson to a close, starting by shuffling papers into order on her clipboard.

Edward's message flashed into her mind, and Z84 realised this could be her chance to get into trouble; she would be in grey the next day, and they could meet and talk in private. Having already worked out an idea in her head – she needed to be brave now; the outcome was unknown.

The philosophy of karate had been instilled within her over many years of training. The martial art is about defence, the empty hand, but this required an attack, not of fists, but words.

"Oi! Fatty! I have just about had enough of you," she shouted across to Miss Citrine. "You and your stupid yellow clothes – you're supposed to be bright and energising. You're definitely not a radiator radiating warmth – you're a big fat drain washing away all our strength."

Miss Citrine's face turned white with anger. With smouldering eyes, she leapt up and slammed her hand hard against a red button by the door. Instantly, an alarm sounded – a piercing shriek tearing through the air.

Before she knew what was happening, two burly men entered the room. Miss Citrine pointed a quivering finger at Z84 who soon found herself in a tight headlock from which there was no escape. The Orderlies dragged her out of the room, kicking and screaming; none of the students moving to help. They all knew the consequences.

Z84 woke to find Edward peering down at her. She blinked hard and pulled away from him. Pain shot through her, and she winced.

"Where am I?" she murmured.

"Don't worry; you're safe now."

With her body complaining, she struggled to sit upright. Edward helped her and then held out a metal cup and two small pills. "These are pain-killers and some water to help you swallow them."

Z84 grimaced and swallowed the proffered capsules.

"They were a bit rough with you, but I managed to get you in here." Edward gestured around him. "You're in solitary confinement for a day or two."

Edward pulled up a stool and settled himself before speaking again. "We don't have much time to talk. I need to tell you the new plan. Cara and Mal have changed it."

"New plan? Why what's happened?" She sipped from the cup and listened.

"They've started Thought Reform, beginning with Jancon. Febcon will be next." He started muttering to himself. "I don't know. These kids shouldn't have to go through this. Not my idea of education."

Her stomach churned. In the debate, the Jancon students showed no emotion, no life in their eyes. This was not their normal behaviour. Nausea threatened, and she swallowed more water to hold it down.

"What do you mean? What's going to happen?"

Edward proceeded to explain to Z84, her eyes widening as she listened. "Once all the students are 15, they start the next phase of Metamorphosis. This is the final stage of maturity before they leave at 18. All the Administrators, Teachers and Orderlies were summoned to a meeting. Trefoil have decided to start Thought Reform now. Through various programmes, each student will go through a process that will enable them to carry out their future role when they leave Zephyr."

"Which is?"

"We're not told the details for security purposes."

"So, what's the new plan?" Z84 asked, leaning against the wall behind her.

"We have to get you out on 1st August and not wait until September. Febcon will be starting their programme of Thought Reform on 10th August. We'll do the same as we'd planned before. You and Z42 will be swapped for two of Augcon."

"What about the other Teardrops? What will happen to those in Febcon?"

"We've only planned for two. We don't have time to make arrangements."

"How will you make the swap, Edward? We can't put them in danger."

"Don't worry about them. I'm taking Z59 and Z25 Augcon to solitary for the changeover. They won't be aware they've missed their special day. No one is told about that until the last minute." Edward's eyes clouded over. "I'm sorry I can't do more. I should have done something long ago, but..." His voice shook. Lowering his head, he pinched the bridge of his nose with slender fingers. He was still for a moment or two, and then setting bony shoulders back, lifting tired eyes said, "Pandora and I will do what we can. The first step is always the hardest."

She nodded. Pandora was the funeral director who had helped them before, someone whom Cara knew. Z84 knew all about first steps: making that momentous decision to infiltrate Zephyr; to climb into a coffin, into the unknown. She was already walking on a path to the truth. The way forward was going to be rocky, but they couldn't go back now. She had come too far to disappear back into the shadows, to be Erin, the girl who stood at the periphery of everything, but to be Erin, the girl who steps out of her comfort bubble and takes a risk.

You learn by making mistakes, her confident inner voice said. It's not about failure or success; you must travel along the failed paths to reach the success you want. Another more insistent voice joined in - *you can't, you're useless, you're stupid*. Z84's resolution to stay strong was pummelled; her resilience leeched out as she fought against her own demons. The positive voice now took over; you have come so far, keep on going. Mentally pushing away her enemies of anxiety and low self-esteem head-on, she declared, "We can do this!"

Edward breathed out hard, deflating like a barrage balloon; it was his turn to surrender. "I don't know. Pandora and I have seen what they're capable of. Trefoil are dangerous; they have so many connections."

"What have you seen?" Z84 urged.

"It wasn't an accident, you know. Jess, Cara's mother, was killed and they made it look like she was drunk at the wheel."

Z84 gasped. "How? What? How do you know all this?"

"Pandora and Jess were close friends. When her son George died, Jess was distraught, as you can imagine. She broke down one day and confided that George was a twin and how she had sold Frankie just after he was born. Jess was determined to get Frankie back. Anyway, Jess didn't drink alcohol – allergic I think – so she certainly wouldn't have been drinking the night she died. At the inquest, the pathologist stated they had discovered large quantities of vodka in her stomach. We think Trefoil had her killed to shut her up."

"That's awful!" An image of Cara came into her mind. Her icy features, the spiky white hair, the cold eyes. "Does Cara and her father suspect any of this? How well does Pandora know them? I don't think we should trust Cara."

"I'm sure we can trust her: she's fighting to get you out of here. Professor Mallory, on the other hand, is a law unto himself." Edward stood and stretched. "I have to go. They'll be wondering where I've got to."

"You can't go... I have so many things I need to ask you... please stay."

"It's too dangerous. I'll be back later with some food. We can talk then. Sleep now while you can." Edward opened the door and went out. The door firmly closed behind him. There was no keyhole or lock to the cell, just a tiny flashing red light indicating it was now locked.

Z84 lay down, her muscles thanking her for the respite, her mind racing, her head full of questions.

Report: 2465

To:　　John Johnson, Joyce Williams, Oliver Irons

From:　Esme Dorling

Jancon Thought Reform has commenced. Interesting
reactions from students. Z11 and Z33 are proving
to be strong in their beliefs. They make excellent
leadership material. My suggestion would be to
speed up their metamorphosis.

Z84 has shown her true colours at last. Her breakdown
has been dealt with. She must undergo Thought Reform
immediately. Suggest 10th August with Febcon.

I look forward to our meeting. I am sure you
will be very pleased with Zephyr's progress.

chapter 5

"You, stupid man! This is all your fault." Stella's shrill words sliced through the open door from the kitchen.

"How, is it my fault?" Patrick's question floated into the room.

"Because you didn't try and stop Erin and Mal."

Miranda squirmed in her seat, listening to the heated discussion going on in the next room. She pulled her knees up to her chest and hid her face, trying to make herself as small as possible. The argument continued.

"What are you going to do now? We can't afford to live here if you're not working. The shop is doing well, and I've had a big order from someone in London which will tide us over for a few months but then..." Stella's voice dripped away.

"I don't know. I've tried all my contacts, but there's nothing. I can't get a job anywhere!"

"This is Erin's fault with her meddling. She wouldn't listen."

"It was bound to happen one day. We have to make the best of it," Patrick soothed.

"Perhaps we should talk to Bianca and Neal. They might have some ideas on what to do. At least their daughter's sensible, unlike Erin. But then we might be putting Petra in danger too. Oh, what a mess!"

"I think we should contact Trefoil…" At the mention of the organisation who ran Zephyr, Miranda uncurled like a cat and crept towards the door to listen more closely.

"What? Are you mad as well as stupid?" Stella was saying.

"Stella, stop shouting at me and listen." Patrick was calm now. "I want to get Erin out of that school. I want my family to be together, as it should be."

"But, we can't, the house, my shop… what will my friends think if we lose everything?"

Patrick's voice rose. "None of that matters if we don't have our family with us. We've lived these lies for so long, and I don't want to continue. I can't let it continue. We can always move abroad, start again."

"You're frightening me, Patrick. We can't do that. Angela warned us not to cause trouble, and now you've lost your job. We'll be penniless again. I can't live like that again."

"Your sister hasn't a clue about families and love. Don't you love your children, Stella?"

Miranda, behind the door, held her breath and waited. *If I hold my breath until she speaks then everything will be fine.*

"Yes, of course I love them. They're part of you and me. I feel like I've lost a limb with Erin gone."

The breath rushed out of Miranda, and she fell against the door, her chest heaving. Chairs scraped as the two adults leapt to their feet.

"What the...? Miranda, have you been listening?" asked Patrick.

"I couldn't help it; you were shouting, and it scared me."

"Everything's fine. You don't need to worry," Stella said, rushing across to her daughter ready to hug her. Miranda flinched, and Stella stopped, holding up her hand, her manicured fingers stretching out like a star.

Miranda reciprocated the gesture, and as their fingers touched, she said, "Please don't argue. I'm sorry you're both sad." She let her hand drop away. "I will go back if that would help. I miss Zephyr; it's the only life I know."

Patrick shook his head. "It's too late for that. You belong here. We love you, Miranda."

"We are one being. We belong here. We are loved." Miranda's eyes clouded over as she intoned the Zephyr mantra three times; her face a blank page, her body frozen. Then, as she uttered the last word, she blinked and looked around.

"What was that?" Patrick whispered.

"I don't know," Stella whispered back. "Miranda, are you okay?"

"Yes, I'm fine; thank you. How are you?" The girl answered, smiling. "Shall I make some tea?"

"I knew I'd find you here." Petra's voice floated on the wind to where Miranda was perched on the altar rock of The Seven Spirits. "Erin loved it here too," she added, plonking herself on the grass.

Miranda just smiled.

"It's so hot!" Petra went on. "The others have gone down to the river to cool off. Do you want to go?"

"No, I can't swim."

"Don't worry; it's really shallow. Anyway, I could teach you."

"It's all right. I don't want to, thank you." Miranda frowned. "Is that okay?"

"'Course it is. You don't have to do things if you don't want to. I'm happy here just chilling."

Miranda grinned then, remembering what Mal had said. "Me too."

The sun was high in the sky, and the two girls were silent for a while, basking in the warmth. The air was still, and the only sound was the drone of traffic edging its way along the sleepy streets of Newton below. Miranda sighed and found her tight muscles begin to give a little. Memories of the boy she had left behind in Zephyr came to her, and a hot ache began to grow in her chest. She missed seeing him every day. Sharp tears pricked her eyes, and she held her breath, willing them not to fall. Is this what love feels like? She mused. I want to see him so much, to touch his hand, to hear his voice. Was that a real feeling, a real emotion?

"I wanted to ask you something?" It was Petra breaking into her thoughts, bringing her back to this new reality.

Miranda scratched her head, enjoying the feel of her hair. It was now a reasonable length – a pixie cut,

Patrick called it – and she loved touching it. "Yes. What would you like to know?"

Petra paused before speaking. "Erin is... was my best friend and I miss her. She told me about my twin sister, and I talked to Mum and Dad about her. Do you know Cassandra?"

"I don't know of anyone with that name. I'm sorry."

"Well, it was a long shot. There's probably loads of kids in your school."

Miranda clambered off the altar stone and knelt near to Petra. "You don't understand. None of us have names, only numbers. What time was she born?"

Petra's eyes narrowed. "I'm not sure, but I think Mum said three minutes past six in the morning; I appeared five minutes later, apparently."

"She could be Z63. I know her. She's a Marcon like me." Miranda studied Petra's face, taking in every feature. "Yes, I can see the resemblance now."

"That's incredible." Petra's face lit up. "Tell me about her. Please."

"I don't know her very well, not like you know your friends here in Newton. We have the same lessons, and I see her in debates and in the Orientation Sector. We can talk then. She's very clever."

"There's so much I don't know." Petra paused. "I didn't believe Erin. I thought she was making it all up, and now she's gone, and I can't say I'm sorry and..." her voice trailed away.

"We're going to get her out," whispered Miranda.

Petra's eyes widened. "What? How? When?" she asked, grabbing Miranda's hands tightly. "I want to help. How can I help?"

Wrenching her hands away and hugging them to her chest, Miranda looked for a moment like a small child who had put her hand too close to a flame. I must do this, she thought. We can't do this by ourselves. We need all the help we can get. Then she spoke. "Mal and I are going down to Cornwall in a couple of days. Once we get Erin out, we can see how we can help the others to escape too. Let's go and talk to him."

"Okay." Petra leapt to her feet and reached out to Miranda, who was inwardly struggling with this simple gesture.

You have come so far, keep on going – the little voice in her head persisted. Taking her new friend's hands, she allowed herself to be pulled up, and they set off back home. A sudden roar of a car engine cut into her reverie, and a shiny red sports car swept into their little road. The girls froze and stared as it pulled up to the gates of Miranda's house. Mal was standing there waiting, and his face broke into a broad grin as Cara extricated herself from the driver's seat and ran to hug him.

"Gorgeous!"

"Me or the car?" squealed Cara.

"Both of you," Mal said, kissing her. Miranda watched them stride arm in arm around the car, Mal stroking the bonnet and sliding his fingers along the chrome, exclaiming as he did so.

"I was left a lot of money by a great aunt I've never met, so I thought I would travel in style and swap the bike for this beautiful beast. Shall we go for a drive?"

"Mal?" Petra shouted across, making the young man glance up. "We need to talk!"

"Hey girls, look at this machine. Isn't she amazing?" Mal beckoned them.

Cara whipped round. The sneer she threw at Miranda was momentary, but the younger girl caught it and held it in her heart. Cara's ice-cold eyes flashed a warning, and then as though a warm fire had been lit, she was suddenly all smiles. "I'm just borrowing him for a bit. See you later, girls." She squeezed herself behind the leather steering wheel, pressed a button and the car revved into life.

Mal looked sheepish and spread his hands, palms out in an unspoken sorry gesture. "Won't be long." Then beaming like a Cheshire cat, he folded himself into the passenger seat.

Keeping back against the wall, Miranda observed Cara skilfully turn the car around and skid off towards the town. Ushering Petra down the driveway towards the house, she pondered on what had just occurred, her inner voice reminding her to take care. We cannot trust her. She betrayed us before and will do it again. Thrusting her hands into the pockets of her jeans, she felt around for the bit of folded paper she placed in there earlier. Holding the paper boat tightly in her grasp like a talisman giving her strength to continue, she vowed she would continue to find the truth for both her and her sister.

Later that evening, tucked up in bed reading, Miranda savoured the experience of having piles of novels to choose from, delving into each book, disappearing into many realms, and adopting new personas. She was steeped in a world inhabited by vampires when a tap at the door became part of that world. Then it became more insistent, jolting her back to reality. The evil creatures faded away, back onto the pages.

"Yes," she said. "Who is it?"

"It's me, Mal. Can I come in?"

Miranda answered with a yes, and the door opened a little to reveal her brother's grinning face, his eyes shining with excitement. "Cara and I have just got back. What a cool car that is!"

"Anyway," he continued, remaining with his fingers curled round the handle. "I've been talking to Dad. He wants to help. I've given him Pandora's number. He's going to come down with us in my car while Cara goes on ahead. The main thing is not to worry. We've got it all planned and hopefully it'll all go smoothly."

"Thanks for letting me know."

Mal closed the door saying, "Sleep well."

Miranda returned to her reading; the vampires now melding into Cara's face.

 Z84 and Z42 stood to attention waiting by the lift doors. 1st August was finally here, and they were ready to put their plan into action. Z84 glanced across to the eight others alongside them, all in wigs and dressed in "nice" clothes as her grandma would say. To her eyes, the clothes were out of fashion. None of the eight commented on Z84 and Z42 being present – they all knew the consequences.

This was the day the Augcon students would see their parents; the end of their five years in the Chrysalis Phase and thus entering their Metamorphosis Phase. This would lead them, over three years, to their Day of Awakening when they turned 18. Yet, only Z84 knew this day was also their fifteenth birthday and that the two people, each student would meet, would be their parents. She longed to tell them. She still felt guilty about the two students with whom they had been swapped. Edward had orchestrated an incident which resulted in the two Augcon students being in the Correction Sector for the whole day. Z84 knew from experience what that might mean for the two of them, but she also recognised that sometimes you had to sacrifice the few for the sake of the many.

This was also the day Edward and Pandora, along with Patrick, Mal and Cara, were going to help them to escape. Absentmindedly, she scratched her head: the black wig made her scalp itch. The map, given to her by Patrick on her arrival to Zephyr, was safely folded and stored in her shoe underneath the ball of her foot. She had added various notes about the inside of Zephyr and what she remembered about the outside and the farm.

The metal doors opened. A rustle behind her and a sharp voice ringing out turned her attention to the man in green, Mr Verde, who was now herding them into the gaping lift space. Taking a deep breath, she too entered and stood silent as a wraith until the doors slid closed and the metal box began to ascend to the surface above.

Three black cars sat in a line. The hanger in which they resided was vast with smooth grey flooring and bright overhead lighting. Z84 found herself being pushed towards one of the cars, and as she climbed in, she saw Z42 was being taken over to another car. Her breathing quickened, and she fought to stay calm. He'll be at the hotel. I'll see him at the hotel. Don't panic; just breathe.

Huge doors opened with a rumble, and the cars rolled out in convoy. Z84 strained to see through the blacked-out glass and could make out the shape of the farmhouse to her right; then it was just fields and moorland until they turned into a tree-lined lane. The cars ground to a halt, gravel crunching, and the doors opened. They had pulled up in front of a beautiful Georgian building, the same hotel as before.

Having gone through the back door the last time, she was keen to see what the main hall would be like and she wasn't disappointed. The ornate, carved ceiling was just the icing on the cake. The floor was a checkerboard pattern of different coloured marble, statues perched on pedestals within domed alcoves and oil paintings adorned creamy-coloured walls.

"Come along now." Professor Hessonite, wearing a bright orange outfit, was hurrying them towards the main restaurant, arms outstretched shepherding them.

We must go now, thought Z84. We must put our trust in Edward and the others.

They were about to enter a room full of tables laid out for lunch with shiny cutlery and glasses catching the sunlight, when she stopped, frozen with fear. She looked around her. I can't see him, where is he?

Someone grabbed her hand from behind and turning she was overjoyed to see the smiling face of Z42. He pulled her away from the line and guided her towards a wide corridor leading towards the back of the building.

"Get back here!" shouted Mr Verde. "No one is to leave."

"She's not feeling very well. I'm just taking her to the toilet," said Z42 ushering Z84 along the corridor. To support his statement, Z84 doubled over as though in agony and heaved, pretending to vomit over the tiled floor.

Professor Hessonite pulled a face at the other teacher. "I'll go and keep an eye on them." She trotted after them, her shoes squeaking on the shiny surface.

Z42 linked arms with Z84 and passing the men's toilets to the left they turned a corner to gain access to the ladies. Edward was there waiting for them in the corridor, hidden from view.

"Hurry! Mal's outside waiting for you," he whispered, and they dashed towards an open door. "I'll deal with her," he said, gesturing towards the orange vision that was just turning the corner.

Freedom beckoned, and the two young people hurried towards it. Outside Mal revved up his little Fiat as soon as they fell into the car and sped off down the driveway towards the main road. "You okay?" he asked them.

"Yes, we're good, thanks. I just hope Edward is able to keep them busy in there." Z84 waved her hand at the hotel that was growing smaller every second.

"He's stronger than he looks. He's swum the English Channel, so this will be a piece of cake for him."

"Really!" Z84 raised her eyebrows and gaped at her brother. "He doesn't look strong enough."

"If everything goes smoothly, we should have a bit of time before anyone gets suspicious."

Erin relaxed once they were on the main road and could see that no one was following them. This is too easy, reflected Z84, I can't believe they haven't missed us. Then, almost as these musings came to her, Z42 cried out from the back seat. "We have company." Z84 whirled around to see in the far distance a black car gaining on them.

Z84 could see Mal's fingers clenching on the steering wheel and sweat forming droplets on his temples. "Don't worry," she whispered.

"I know. We're nearly there. I'm going to drop you off at the Necklace of Stones. You'll need to cross the moor on foot to reach the stones and then keep on going. Pandora is expecting you. She's in the car park." Then as an afterthought, he added, "In a hearse."

The road curled around and thankfully hid them from view as Mal pulled over and the two fugitives tumbled out. "I'll see you at Cara's. Take care."

"You too!" Z84 shouted, slamming the door and following Z42 up the grassy bank. Hiding behind shrubs and bushes, they watched their pursuers tail the little white Fiat. "I hope he's not in danger," she said, crossing her fingers.

"He'll be fine," Z42 answered. Z84 gave him a sidelong glance; he seemed amazingly calm for someone who had never been out of Zephyr.

In unison, they turned towards the vast expanse of the moor where several huge craggy rocks stood vertical, creating three separate circles in a line. Just like the Spirits back home, thought Z84 and immediately felt an affinity for this ancient place.

Skirting round the Necklace of Stones, they soon reached the car park and the hearse with glass panels through which Z84 glimpsed a coffin and flowers in the shape of the letters MUM. Pandora leaning against the glossy, black vehicle was looking at her watch repeatedly and then scanning the horizon. Her face lit up when they scurried towards her, and she rushed to open the passenger door. Z42 and Z84 piled into the front seats, and while Pandora hit the ignition and then the accelerator, they threw on black jackets over their clothes. Z84 pulled off the hated wig, opened the window wide and threw it into some bushes. She gave her head a good scratch before donning a black top hat.

"There isn't a body in there." Pandora indicated the coffin with a toss of her head. "It's all for show."

"Thank goodness for that," Z84 said, pulling on her seat belt and clicking it into place before settling into the slate-grey leather seat.

A hearse isn't the fastest of getaway cars but wouldn't be suspected of being one. That was what they had all hoped, anyway. It swept smoothly down the driveway towards the main road and then indicated to turn left.

The journey should only take about half an hour to get to Castleton, but you can't hurry a hearse unless you want to look suspicious. Pandora drove at a sedate 30 miles per hour, and they finally entered the little town nestling around the castle remains, high on a hill. Passing the Tourist Information Centre and Post Office, she reduced speed even further and then indicated to turn right into Little Street. The hearse pulled up outside number ten, and Pandora turned off the engine. It ticked rhythmically as the car cooled.

They were parked outside a terrace of houses with bay windows. The front door opened, and a grey-haired man stood on the threshold. His face solemn, he looked like he was about to intone a mass as he proceeded to bring his hands together as in prayer. Z84 followed Z42 up the slate path.

"My boy!" exclaimed the man, clapping his gnarled hands together in rapture, his dark eyes shining. "Welcome, welcome. Do come in," he sang out, standing back with a theatrical flourish of his arms. "I have been expecting you."

Pandora followed them in and closed the door firmly behind her. "Were you followed?" the man asked. The two young people stared at him. "Oh, dear, where are my manners? Goodness me. I am Professor Mallory, Cara's father. You must be Erin?" he said, proffering a hand towards Z84. She took it, and a firm, smooth grip encompassed her fingers.

He turned to Z42 then. "...and you are... Frankie. My son." Tears began to slide down the old man's pale cheeks. The young man gasped, his eyes wide with shock.

"You must be mistaken, sir."

The professor recovered himself, blew his nose loudly on a patterned silk handkerchief he pulled from the top pocket of his velvet jacket, and said in his mellow, melodic voice. "Well, we can talk about that later. Let's get you safe first." He guided them along a wide hall and then down some steps which led into a large kitchen. It looked out onto a sloping garden, full of rose bushes.

Pandora scurried over to the kettle and busied herself, making coffee while the two young people sat down at the scrubbed oak table set in the centre of the room. A sudden heat washed over Z84, and the room spun around her. She cradled her head in her hands and waited for it to pass. A door above them opened and slammed shut. Z84 tilted her head to listen. The sound of someone's feet striking the floor could be heard, making their way towards them, down the steps.

A breathless figure appeared in the doorway. Her pink and white spiky hair seemed to glow from the hall light behind. Her ice-blue eyes shone as she announced, "I've just come from the hospital. They pushed Mal's car right off the road and left him for dead."

At this, Z84 leapt to her feet, the chair skittering back across the tiled floor, and grabbed Cara with both hands. "You!" she screamed. "What have you done to my brother! This is your fault!" She pushed the startled woman against the door frame and proceeded to attack her face and arms.

A deep voice came from the stairwell, and Erin froze with one arm raised to hit Cara again. "Stop this now! You won't help Mal by fighting."

Turning, she saw a familiar figure and fell into his arms. "Dad! Oh, Dad, thank goodness."

Patrick pulled her close. "I promised to always be there for you. I love you, Erin."

TREFOIL HQ

Transcript from meeting

John Johnson: You, Esme Dorling have failed yet again to keep watch over your brood. Explain yourself.

Esme Dorling: I apologise most humbly. In my defence, I have done everything in my power to continue our work at Zephyr. Only two students have…

Oliver Irons: We don't want to lose any of them. We have invested millions into this project NN2000. We cannot fail.

Esme Dorling: Please give me one more chance. We have people looking for the two students, Z59 and Z25 Augeon.

Joyce Williams: You are more stupid than you look! They swapped with Z84 and Z42 – Erin Winslow and Franklyn Mallory.

Esme Dorling: I was not aware of that. We will focus on finding them.

Oliver Irons: This is your final chance, Dorling. Do not let us down!

Chapter 6

Miranda huddled on a chair, one of many sitting forlorn and empty, waiting for people who were concerned for their loved ones. The white walls and endless corridors of Castleton Hospital reminded her of Zephyr; the clean, antiseptic smell invading her nostrils at every turn, calming her. She was alone.

Patrick and Cara had remained at the hospital until they knew Mal was out of danger and then left Miranda to her vigil. Patrick was keen to see Erin; Cara wanted to see her father.

The television, in the waiting room, displayed various characters arguing with each other, and she gazed blankly at the text appearing on the screen. It reminded her of the arguments she had overheard between Patrick and Stella. Since then the last few days had passed in a whirl with them travelling down to Cornwall and Mal and Pandora helping Erin and Z42 to escape. Unfortunately, it ended with Mal being whisked off to hospital in an ambulance leaving his little car, now a complete wreck, overturned in a ditch.

A young nurse had been kind towards them all when Mal had been admitted; showing them where to wait. Hours passed before a doctor, looking drawn and hollow-eyed, appeared in front of them and explained the injuries looked a lot worse than they actually were. Mal had been moved to a ward: tubes and wires still attached to his body and was asleep when the three of them were finally allowed to see him. Miranda, looking down at the prone figure, breathed deeply trying to encourage him to keep breathing too. She didn't want to lose him.

Now, staring at the plain wall beyond, Miranda wondered if it had all been worth it. This was all due to him wanting to save his sisters.

The creaking of a chair made her break from her reverie. An elderly couple were sitting down on the opposite side of the room. The man patted his wife's hand while she sobbed into a sodden tissue. Miranda refused to give into tears. I must stay strong for Mal, she thought.

"Miss Winslow?" A lilting, gentle voice came from nowhere, and Miranda turned her head to see a lady dressed in a blue uniform. "Would you like to see your brother now? He's asking for you."

Miranda followed the nurse in a daze. Entering the ward, they passed a reception desk with staff talking in hushed tones and several beds lined up along the wall, each one occupied with a man or boy in various states of illness. There at the end lay a pale figure; dark hair pressed into the soft pillow. Approaching the bed, Miranda was pleased to see a lot of tubes and wires had been removed but shocked to see the bruises and cuts peppering his youthful face.

Mal struggled to sit up.

"Oh no, you don't young man. We'll have none of that, thank you very much." The nurse spoke with authority and a hint of kindness. She patted the chair at the side of the bed. "You sit here and talk some sense into him, love. He's very poorly and needs plenty of rest."

As soon as she had gone, Mal leaned over, grasping the bedsheets to give him more leverage. "Are they safe?"

"Yes, I think so. Patrick and I waited with Cara as planned. We saw you drop them off at the Necklace of Stones and followed you at a distance." Miranda paused. "How are you? The nurse said you'd broken some ribs."

Mal's chest was bound tightly with bandages while a long livid cut on his forehead was held together by stitches. His face, normally tanned from the sun, bore a greenish tinge, and dark shadows encircled his eyes, yet he tried to make light of the situation. "Yeah. I've had worse playing rugby, but they're keeping me in overnight for monitoring."

Miranda knew there was more to it than that. Terrifying memories clouded her mind. They had found him hanging upside-down, unconscious – hardly breathing. The metallic aroma of blood drifting through a fractured window. The engine clicking sadly, whiling away the minutes until the emergency services arrived. Thankfully, the airbag had popped out and was cushioning his body against the steering wheel.

Now, in the safe, sterile world of Castleton Hospital, Mal patted her hand. "You should've seen the other guy!" he said chuckling and then doubled over with pain, clutching his chest. After a few minutes composing himself, he lay back against the pillows.

"We came over the brow of a hill and saw your car in a ditch. I thought you were dead." The enormity of it all suddenly hit Miranda like a sledgehammer, and fat tears rolled down her cheeks. "The firefighters had to cut you out of your little car."

"I loved that car." Mal looked downcast for a moment and then his face brightened when Miranda spoke.

"They're all at Cara's house. Patrick's going to visit later this evening."

"You mean, Dad..."

Miranda nodded. She still found it difficult to accept she had parents or a family, yet she was starting to love this young man. An image of Mal being pulled out of his broken car brought another rush of emotion coursing through her. She gingerly took his hand, tanned against her pale one, and placed her free hand on top.

"You're safe now," she said. "The doctors and nurses will take care of you. We thought it had been an accident until we saw the guards just drive off; their car nearly collided with us when they sped back up the hill! We left the police studying the black tyre trails crisscrossing the road. I think they were trying to kill you."

"I don't remember very much. I remember picking up Erin and the boy. The rest is a fog. Perhaps it wasn't a great plan after all," sighed Mal yawning.

"You go to sleep, I'll just sit here," Miranda said, letting go of his hand and making herself as comfortable as she could on the hard hospital chair. It was going to be a long night.

An insistent thumping at the front door caused Erin to pull apart from her father's embrace. Her heart hammered against her ribcage as though it wanted to escape. "They've found us!" she cried.

"Don't worry. I'll go and see who it is," Professor Mallory announced, his calm countenance had a softening effect on Erin. "Cara, you must hide them." He hurried out.

Cara glared, her eyes frozen, cheeks still blazing from where Erin had hit her. She threw accusations at his retreating back. "Dad, why should I? Why should I help her? She's a pain in the neck!"

"Wait!" a loud voice came from across the room. It was Z42. Cara whirled round.

"Are you my sister?"

"Frankie? Is it really you?" Cara said, rushing over to the young man extending her arms to hug him. Z42 took a step back and held up his hand like a starfish, his eyes wild with sudden fear.

Stopping before him, Cara held out her hand, and their fingers touched. Z42's face held a brief smile until yelling from the room above broke the moment. The words were indistinct, but it sounded threatening.

"They've found us!" Erin repeated. "Please help, Cara. I'm sorry about before. Please…"

The shouting overhead and the loud thuds of many feet spurred Cara into action. Opening a huge fridge door, she pressed a hidden mechanism which caused the interior to swing back to reveal a flight of stairs leading downwards. "Quick, both of you. You too, Patrick."

"What about Pandora?" Erin said, looking across at the woman who had helped them to escape.

"Don't worry about me. Go quickly now!"

Z42 lead the way down the gloomy stone steps; Erin and her father racing after him. Entering a small box of a room caused a light to flicker on, illuminating the interior, and started up a whirr of air conditioning, adding a chill to the airless, musty space. Chairs and blankets, even a mini-fridge and TV, placed around the room made it look almost homely.

Erin strained to hear what was happening above them and was rewarded with the distant bang of doors slamming shut. They were trapped. She swallowed hard and took some deep breaths. The air was now sweet and clean, and she found the tension she had held so hard in her shoulders begin to loosen. She was aware of her dad pacing around the room, a haunted look on his face.

"We'll be all right, Dad," she said.

"I know. I'm just so frustrated I let us all get in this situation in the first place."

"You weren't to know. You were just doing the best for your family. Come and sit down and I'll see what's in this little fridge." Erin was thankful to be doing something and glanced across at her friend. "Z42... Frankie...?"

The young man who had been so strong in Zephyr was now crumpled in a heap on the floor, and she hurried over to him. "I... they... Family... I can't..." He spoke so quietly, Erin struggled to hear every word.

"What is it? What's wrong?" she asked, rubbing his shoulder to give comfort. He cringed from her touch and then even more disturbing, he began to howl like a wolf with eyes blazing and teeth bared.

"Dad! Help me. What's wrong with him?" Erin cried out.

Patrick was at the boy's side in a flash. "I was afraid this might happen." He spoke soothing words to Frankie, who was now sitting in a foetal position, rocking and muttering.

"Get some water, love. I have a sedative here; it'll help him to sleep."

It took both of them to administer the sleeping tablets with Frankie thrashing his arms around, shouting and spitting. Eventually, he settled down on a blanket Erin had placed on the floor. When his eyes finally closed, she covered him with another blanket and while Patrick carefully lifted Frankie's head, tucked a cushion underneath.

Erin fell into one of the chairs, exhausted, then curling her legs under her, she leaned her elbow on the arm of the chair and rested her head. Patrick pulled out two bottles of water from the mini-fridge and passed one to her. He glugged his water back and then, after wiping his mouth on the back of his hand, said, "Miranda was just the same when she first came home. I don't know what's going on in that school, but it takes a while for the kids to become accustomed to the outside. Your sister had nightmares for weeks."

"Where is she now?" Erin had been so caught up with everything else she hadn't thought of Miranda. She immediately felt cold and hot at the same time. "Is she safe?"

Patrick explained that Miranda was at the hospital with Mal. Erin listened while she sipped her drink then contemplating what they should do next, she remembered the map folded inside her shoe. Drawing it out, Erin handed it to her father.

"I've added what I can. I've superimposed details onto the old map you gave me."

Patrick glanced at it and then stuffed it in his pocket. "This'll be useful. Miranda and Frankie can add more detail to it when they get a chance."

Erin thought over the last few hours. I'm not sure if we've done the right thing bringing Frankie out. Mal's badly hurt too, and I can't imagine what could be going on upstairs. Can we trust Cara and her dad to protect us?

An image of a nice old lady, a stranger, sitting on a bench in a churchyard, swam in front of her. It had been back in March, after seeing Miranda for the first time. She had been trying to tell Petra, on the phone, about her twin sister, but she wouldn't listen. In her frustration, Erin had ended up running away to seek solace and Elsie had come to her rescue.

The image of Elsie was fading, yet the memory of lavender perfume and the feel of the lacy handkerchief wiping away her tears was strong. What was it she said after Mal and Cara had found her in the churchyard? Closing her eyes to concentrate, Elsie's voice came to her. Watch that one. If she's like her father, I wouldn't trust her. It was a warning. Elsie had told her she had worked with Professor Mallory in some laboratory. That was how she knew him and why she recognised Cara.

"Dad?"

"Yes, love."

"Do you trust them? Cara and her father?"

"I think so. We don't have many who can help us. Besides, Frankie is Professor Mallory's son. He wouldn't hurt him."

"How do we know that? He says so, but he might not be."

"What do you suggest we do? Look at this place! We can't get out without help."

At this, Erin's eyes searched the ceiling and walls for clues, but the room was completely solid, apart from the steps leading up to the back of the fridge. No doors or windows adorned the walls. Nothing could get in or out without coming through the hidden door. Erin jumped up and crossed the room. She climbed the steps sliding her hands along the smooth walls. "There has to be a way out."

Patrick copied his daughter, but they soon came to the same conclusion - they were imprisoned.

Returning to their cell, Patrick put his arms around Erin. "Sweetheart, we have to trust them for now. Get some rest, and I'll keep watch."

He kissed the top of her head, and she mumbled an agreement through a wide yawn. It was true, she was exhausted, and there was nothing they could do. Erin slumped onto the chair, her eyelids now growing heavy. She battled to keep them open, only to lose the fight. Erin dozed, fitting her head against the back of the armchair and snuggling into a soft cushion.

It seemed like only minutes when Patrick woke her, but it was an hour in real-time. She stretched her arms wide and looked across at Frankie, who lay like a dead man on the floor. An occasional snort escaped from his nose, reminding them he was still alive.

Patrick held his forefinger to his lips and whispered, "I heard something." A sharp click resonated from the top of the stairs and seconds later footsteps could be heard on the stonework.

Erin was instantly alert. Tension returned to her muscles, but this time it served a purpose. She would be ready for what or who was coming to find them.

ZEPHYR SCHOOL

Bulletin

To: All Teachers, Administrators and Orderlies

From: Principal Dorling

You have allowed two students to escape our school. This is unacceptable. When I discover who has helped them that person will be terminated from the project. You are all at risk.

You MUST be vigilant in all your duties. The Orderlies will carry out a thorough search of Zephyr.

Chapter 7

 Miranda was amazed by the array of food and drinks available at the café in the hospital. She shuffled forwards as the queue snaked towards the counter. It all looks so delicious, she thought. One of the nurses had suggested she went to find something to eat while Mal slept, promising she would watch him. She was glad she had agreed: her stomach was now rumbling.

"How can I help you?" The young man, behind the glass cases, beamed at her.

"I'm not sure. What would you recommend?"

"The coffee is particularly good. I don't drink it myself though; it's bad for my heart."

"Thank you, Trainee," Miranda said, having seen the man's badge. "I'll have some tea then; I don't want to hurt my heart."

He laughed, taking a cardboard cup and filling it with steaming hot water. "That's not my name by the way. I'm Dillon. Anyway, what kind of tea? We have all sorts." He began to list them all before Miranda stopped him.

"Please, just tea." She couldn't deal with all this information.

He rubbed his chest, "I have a heart problem."

"Really? You look so healthy."

"Yeah, I'm okay as long as I keep on taking the tablets." He placed the cup onto the counter before Miranda. "Cake? We have all kinds – chocolate, lemon, ginger…"

Miranda held up her hand to halt his flow of words. "Anything will do. Thank you."

After fumbling with coins, which were becoming more familiar, Miranda finally made her way out of the café and, being careful not to spill her drink, walked back along the corridor to Mal's ward. She was worried she had left him alone for too long.

Behind the long reception desk, various people stood or sat, some looking at computer screens, others studying clipboards. No one took any notice as she wandered back into the long room full of beds. It was quiet, one or two patients had visitors speaking in hushed voices, many were sleeping, and one or two had curtains pulled around them. An intermittent beep from a monitor was almost restful.

Looking down at the cardboard tray with the cup and cake, Miranda, her tummy now growling with anticipation, realised she was looking forward to the food. She was thinking of the young man at the café and how you can never tell what someone is going through when she saw there was a nurse standing over Mal's bed. Not wanting to disturb them, Miranda decided to wait near the closed curtains of the adjacent bed and watched the nurse tap the drip and check the monitor.

The person was dressed head to toe in bright orange and talking, her head bowed. Miranda looked back towards the reception desk; all the people there were in blue or white - no one wore orange. The woman raised her head, and Miranda stifled a gasp. It was Professor Hessonite from Zephyr. What's she doing here? Mal could be in danger. Should I call someone?

Watching from her vantage point, she could hear part of their conversation. Mal seemed to be asking questions about Zephyr, and the teacher was replying in muted tones while she stalked around the bed to take a seat. Miranda could see her brother was becoming distressed, waving his hands around and coughing and spluttering. Professor Hessonite handed him a plastic glass with some unknown orange liquid inside, holding a straw to his dry lips.

"Stop!" shouted Miranda rushing across so fast her cup upended in its little tray splashing hot tea across the bedsheets. The cake flew over the spotless floor. She skidded on the thick gooey icing and fell hard against the bed. "Don't drink it!" she shouted and two faces, both with eyes and mouths wide with shock, turned towards her.

"Get away from him!" Miranda continued to shout across at the woman, pawing at the drink and then knocking it from her outstretched hand. Mal was still coughing and doubled over in pain.

"Please, don't... please..." He was struggling to breathe now.

"That's enough. Out of our way." A clipped voice came from behind Miranda, and she found herself being pushed roughly to one side, her arm hitting the bedside cabinet in the process. The nurse, dressed in a blue uniform, administered a quick injection and Mal lay still apart from his chest rising and falling rhythmically.

Miranda, nursing her bruised arm, was told to sit quietly. She did so, meek as a young child and watched while the nurse checked the folder, tutting and ticking.

Professor Hessonite stood some distance from the bed, observing the whole process. Her hooded eyes glowered across at Miranda, then she said, "Z89."

"I am not a number; I am Miranda."

"Sorry, Miranda…"

The girl stopped rubbing her arm. Was she hearing correctly? A teacher apologising!

"…it was just orange juice." The woman was continuing to speak. "I was only trying to help Malachi."

Miranda stared at Professor Hessonite and then at her brother.

"It's okay. I tried to tell you, sis," Mal mumbled through dry lips. "She's on our side."

 Erin gestured to her dad to stand to the right side of the entrance while she did the same to the left, masking themselves from whoever entered the room. Only Frankie was visible, and he was still snoring.

The footsteps stopped just outside the room. Erin wrinkled her nose at the strange chemical smell invading her space. It reminded her of death and brought back memories of the science lab at school. The person in the shadows was silent apart from a laborious breathing. A rustle of material, a sharp intake of breath and a cry accompanied the hooded figure who was now creeping in towards Frankie.

With a nod, Erin threw herself at the shoulders of the person while Patrick rugby tackled them to the ground.

"GET OFF ME!" The figure shouted, flailing their arms around. "It's me, you idiots!"

Patrick pulled back the black hood exposing a woman's face. "Pandora! Thank goodness, it's you," he said, leaning back against a wall, his chest heaving. "What's with all the creeping about? I nearly hit you."

Pandora sat, her legs and arms akimbo, her dark curly hair dishevelled, her black funeral suit in disarray. "I really must stop opening things," she laughed. "You never know what you might find."

Erin studied the woman and then dissolved into laughter. "You're crazy," she said, wiping her eyes.

"What's going on?" The tussle had woken Frankie who was now leaning up on one elbow peering at the three people piled up on the floor.

Erin crawled over to him and stretched out her hand. He touched her fingers and smiled. "Welcome back," she said.

The woman in black was now clambering to her feet and straightening her clothes. "We don't have much time. We need to get going. I'll explain in the car."

They followed Pandora up the steps, out through the fridge and into the large homely kitchen. Erin could make out stars studding the inky night sky above as they hurried through a conservatory, full of exotic looking plants, to the garden beyond.

Pandora opened a wooden door, hidden in a high brick wall surrounding the garden. They all piled into the waiting vehicle, hidden from view, no streetlights and no nosy neighbours.

"What happened back there?" Patrick asked, putting on his seat belt.

"Where's Cara?" asked Erin, secretly hoping something awful had happened to her.

Pandora, remaining mute, drove through narrow streets. Erin could see the frown of concentration on the woman's face reflected in the rear-view mirror.

Finally, they left the town behind, and as the lanes twisted and turned, Pandora began to describe what she had seen.

"I watched Cara take you to the safe room and then I left through the back door. I returned the hearse to the funeral directors' garage and picked up my own car. Sorry, it's a bit of a squeeze. There's usually only me." Erin and Frankie were squashed in the back of the mini and on each bend of the road, which Pandora seemed to take at speed, their legs banged together, causing Frankie to become quite distressed.

"I left as they said you'd be okay, but I had this uneasy feeling in my stomach, so I came back. When I arrived, there was no one at the house. Cara and her dad have vanished."

"What do you mean vanished?" Patrick asked through gritted teeth.

"Exactly that. There was no sign of them. The front door was wide open. I called out, but no one answered."

"Do you know who came to the house?" Frankie interjected, holding onto the back of the driver's seat as they whizzed round yet another twist in the lane.

"I'm not sure, but they left this." Pandora brandished a card which Erin plucked from her hand.

She passed it to Patrick who snorted with derision. "Trefoil. Who else could it have been? What was the state of the house like?"

"They had obviously made a thorough search of the place, drawers open, contents strewn all over the place."

"Trefoil have taken Cara and her father. They might be in danger," Patrick said.

"Oh, I think they'll be able to handle themselves!" Erin exclaimed.

"What do you mean?" asked Pandora, changing gear as they came to a junction.

"Nothing," answered Erin. "Just a feeling."

They turned right, and soon passed a pub positioned squarely by the side of the road. An illuminated large white sign announced 'The Coach and Horses: bar snacks and main meals available'. Turning left off the main road, the lane became very narrow, and the little car jumped around as it hit potholes and cracks in the tarmac.

Turning left off the main road, the lane became very narrow, and the little car jumped around as it hit potholes and cracks in the tarmac.

Eventually, Pandora pulled onto a gravel drive and switched off the engine. She climbed out and then helped the others to extricate themselves. "Welcome to my humble abode," she said, unlocking the front door of a white cottage. "It's not much, but you should be safe here for a while at least." A flick of a switch illuminated a compact room with squashy chairs and a sofa facing an inglenook fireplace. There were flowers everywhere: pink roses in pots, sunflowers in vases, purple heather in jam-jars and even tiny, white daisies protruded from an egg cup.

"I have to get away from death somehow," Pandora said, pulling them into the room and pushing them into the vacant chairs.

She bustled about checking they were alright and then disappeared into the kitchen. Erin leaned back against the floral-patterned cushions and kicked off her shoes. She was still wearing the dress she had been given at Zephyr, but it was decidedly grubby now. I can't wait to get back in my jeans and Vans, she thought. Exhaustion washed over her, her eyes grew heavy, and her head drooped.

The sound of car doors opening, and slamming shut outside in the still of the night caused her to jerk awake. Without warning, Pandora shot past her and galloped to the door. "What? Who is it?" Erin called, stumbling to the window. "No, it can't be... how did she find us?" She whirled around and shouted at Frankie. "It's Professor Hessonite! They must have followed us here. Quick we need to hide. Dad, help us!" Patrick just crossed his legs in answer and smiled at her panic. "Dad, please..."

Pandora flung the door open, and Mal hobbled in supported by the professor.

"Mal!" Erin ran to her brother and hugged him tight until he shouted for her to get off as he was in a lot of pain. Between them, they managed to sit him down on the sofa and make him comfortable. After fussing over Mal, Erin stood to one side, and there was Miranda. They held out their hands in unison and touched the tips of their fingers. "Hello, you," she said grinning.

"Hello," replied Miranda and then to Erin's amazement, she wrapped her arms around her in an enormous hug.

"Z89?" a hesitant voice came from a chair by the fireplace.

Miranda looked up and smiling she went across to the boy from Zephyr. They both made a teardrop shape with their fingers and holding their hands together, formed a butterfly.

"I must get back," Professor Hessonite said, walking towards the door. "The taxi driver's waiting for me."

"Thank you, Amber. We couldn't have done this without you and Edward." Patrick and Pandora were shaking hands with the woman in orange while Erin looked on; her mind whirling, trying to take it all in. So many questions, so much to know and understand.

Once the front door was closed, Erin wanted answers but didn't know where to start. Instead, she fell into a chair and just stared at all the people around her. My brain can't take this all in... I'm so tired...

"I could do with a drink." This was Pandora heading back into the kitchen. "Anyone else?" She called.

"Nothing for me," Patrick answered. "I think it's time you lot got some rest. We'll talk in the morning. I'm sure you have a lot of questions." Mal groaned at this. "Right, young man, let's get you to bed. Pandora has a spare room where you and I can sleep. Everyone else will just have to kip down here."

Being as gentle as he could, he helped Mal to his feet, and they struggled up the stairs. Pandora appeared with a glass of red wine and gulped most of it down. "There are blankets over there," she said, pointing to a pile of bedclothes. "We have a lot to do tomorrow. Sleep tight." And with this, she disappeared up the stairs.

Miranda insisted Erin slept on the sofa while she and Frankie took an armchair each. With the lights extinguished, they settled down for the night. The soft silky darkness enveloped them all and held them until the light of the morning flooded through the flowery curtains.

Report: 2466

To: Esme Dorling

From: John Johnson, Joyce Williams, Oliver Irons

- Traffic accident resulted in one male taken to
  hospital. Believed to be Malachi Winslow.
  Castleton Hospital have informed us he has
  been discharged.

- Professor Mallory's residence was thoroughly
  searched. No one has been discovered there.
  The Mallorys are helping us with our enquiries.

- One red sports car has been returned to Trefoil.

- Any further information, concerning the
  whereabouts of the 2 missing students, Z84 and
  Z42, to be sent immediately.

"No, sorry. That's a worry. Why would a 15-year-old girl die? It was probably one of their inhumane experiments. I said they were corrupt!" The young man pushed himself off the chair and stretched each of his limbs in turn.

Pandora appeared from the hallway. "Good - you're all awake. Let's eat, and then we can talk and plan our next move. Patrick and I need to get you up to speed." She flung back the curtains and sunshine poured in. "There's some clothes in there you can change into," she added, indicating a brown suitcase propped against the door frame.

Later, sitting on a small patio, Miranda savoured the view of the sea. The dark blue water lay between an enormous cliff to the right and two triangular shaped hills to the left. She recognised it as Porthcragen. Patrick and Stella had brought her here after she had left Zephyr. Pandora's little cottage, white-washed walls bright in the summer sun, nestled into the side of a hill which grew into craggy cliffs. Her garden, just like her living room, was abundant with flowers of every colour. The beds surrounded an oval of grass where a large stone toadstool sat; a delicate butterfly fluttering its shimmering blue wings on top of the moss-covered dome. She smiled remembering the butterfly she had helped to escape, and the butterfly brooch Mal had returned to her. Her gaze fell onto her twin who, at that moment, had a mouthful of toast and was spluttering crumbs as she spoke with Patrick. What will the future bring us all? She pondered. There was so much to do and yet so much danger.

"Z89? What do you think?" It was Frankie asking the question. She hadn't heard the earlier part of the discussion, but she knew in her mind what she needed to say now.

"I'm not a number; I'm Miranda. We don't need our numbers anymore. Z84 is Erin and you..." She hesitated.

"Cara and Professor Mallory called me Frankie. Is that my name?"

"I'm not sure. Who visited you at the five-year phases? Patrick and Stella visited me and called me Miranda, and then I discovered they were my...my family." She smiled across to Patrick, who returned a warm grin.

"Two people would visit – both elderly and grey-haired - I never knew their names, but they did call me Frankie. Perhaps they're my family. I'm confused because the professor said, 'my son', but I've never seen him or Cara before."

"We'll find out who they are; don't you worry. We'll call you Frankie if that's okay with you?" said Patrick, lifting a mug to his lips. Frankie nodded. They all continued eating, each one of them lost in their own thoughts.

"It might help if we explain to you what's been happening, to put you all in the picture. We need to plan our next move," Pandora said, collecting up the breakfast things. "You can't stay here forever; we need to get going once Mal is strong enough. I'll just go and check on him. He might be awake now." She hurried into the house.

Patrick took over. "As you know, I lost my job and couldn't find anything of the same level of pay. Trefoil have leant on people to stop me working as punishment for allowing Erin into Zephyr."

Erin gasped. "It wasn't your fault, Dad. We did this, not you."

"Well, in a strange way, being given the sack helped me make up my mind. I had to do something to save my family. We were never told in the beginning the truth behind the school and what it would mean for Miranda. The last fifteen years have been absolute torture for your mum and me." He paused and rubbed his bearded chin - his eyes full of sadness - then continued.

"Stella and I had a long talk, and we decided we would fight for justice, not just for you, but also for children from other families." He stopped to allow Pandora to take her place again. "We met with Petra's mum and dad, Bianca and Neal, and each of us has agreed on the best way forward."

"Which is…?" asked Erin.

Miranda looked across at her. "Shhh! Listen to Patrick."

"Pandora?" Patrick nodded to the woman, who today was dressed in a brightly coloured summer dress, quite different from her usual attire.

"Mal's still asleep," Pandora explained. "Your dad contacted me. Mal told him how I had helped you before, and I agreed we could pull together, each of us using our different skills and knowledge."

"What about Professor Hessonite? Are you sure we can trust her?" Frankie asked.

"I've known Amber for a long time," announced Pandora. "Castleton is quite a small place, and in my line of business, you get to know a lot of people. She's become increasingly disenchanted with Zephyr's methods. She was told it was a new innovative way to educate our young people. They even made her sign the Official Secrets Act."

"Okay," Miranda said. "What do we do now?"

Patrick leaned forward and rested his elbows on his knees. "The next step is to rescue the Teardrops." He waited while that information sank in.

Frankie grinned. "Now, you're talking."

"We believe there are about 12 of them. Is that right, Frankie?"

"Yes."

"What about Z63?" asked Erin, concerned about her new friend.

"Is that Cassandra, Petra's sister?" Miranda asked. Erin nodded.

"That'll be thirteen then." Patrick poured himself another coffee from the glass coffee-pot on the patio table.

"Unlucky for some," said Pandora.

"What ideas have you got? When do we start?" said Erin.

"We've already started," said Patrick. "We sent a drone over the area above Zephyr and took some pictures." He pulled out his laptop and switching it on, he added, "we've located the air vents. I'll show you the aerial images."

They crowded round the screen as Patrick fiddled with various buttons on the keyboard. Pandora took up the explanation. "You can see there's a wood covering this area." As she spoke, she pointed out the trees on the screen. "And, if you look very closely, you can pick out lots of circles on the ground. Here... here and here..." She indicated several silvery circular shapes within the foliage.

"These are the air vents," explained Patrick.

"So? What good is that?" asked Erin.

"We can pump gas in through the vents," Frankie said in a hushed tone.

"But that will kill them, won't it?"

Patrick was very patient. "Edward and Amber have arranged for all the Teardrops to have breathing apparatus when we administer the gas. It will send everyone else to sleep for two hours. That should be enough time to get them out."

Miranda counted up in her head the amount of breathing apparatus they would need. Twelve Teardrops, plus Edward and Z63 and Professor Hessonite. "That makes fifteen," she announced. "That's a lot of equipment to get hold of."

Patrick nodded. "Don't forget, we also need some for those of us going inside Zephyr to bring them out. We'll need at least five. Mal's injured so he can't go in."

"What? I'm fine." A voice from the doorway caused them all to turn. Mal stood there, hair tousled from sleep. Erin was on her feet in an instant and ran to him. They embraced before she led him to an empty seat.

Mal winced on sitting down and cradled his chest with one arm. "Just give me a couple of days. I'll be there."

"We'll see," said Patrick.

Miranda leaned forward. "Where are you going to get this equipment from?"

Erin leaned forward too. "The gas – how are you going to get a sleeping gas?"

It was Pandora who answered them in a clear voice. "I have contacts at the mortuary, at the local hospital. We've managed to collect enough crystals for the whole of Zephyr to sleep for two hours, just as Patrick said."

"Yes, Pandora knows a lot of people," Patrick agreed. "Amber, Professor Hessonite, has ordered the breathing equipment online and it's been delivered to her in Zephyr. She's told Miss Dorling she needs them for a science experiment."

"What about ours?" Frankie asked eagerly.

"Neal's ordered some for us, and it's all arriving tomorrow."

"This is really happening, isn't it!" Erin, with her grey eyes wide, exclaimed.

Patrick nodded assent. A sudden breeze brushed the garden, flowers bobbed their heads, and the blue butterfly took off, twisting his wings into the wind.

Miranda looked again at the screen of the laptop. "What are those larger glass circles?" she asked, pointing them out to the others.

Pandora explained. "They're light columns. They allow natural light to shine down into the space below."

"That will be into the Central Hub, I should think," said Miranda. "That's where the main offices are."

Patrick continued. "We'll need your knowledge of the school to find the Teardrops. We also have Erin's map of the inside of Zephyr. The good news is that Neal, Petra's father, has been working on hacking the Zephyr computer system." He turned towards Frankie. "He's managed to contact Z11, your second in command of The Teardrops."

"There isn't anyone of that number in the Teardrops," whispered Erin. "I think we might have a problem."

Over the next few days, Patrick and Pandora explained their plans, Frankie, Miranda and Erin chipping in with suggestions and improvements. After all, they had lived in Zephyr. Eventually, they developed a plan they were all happy with. Everyone knew what their role would be and what was expected of them.

The breathing equipment was delivered and tested with care; Patrick hired a minibus to transfer them all to a safe house in Shropshire, organised by Petra's mother, Bianca. Meanwhile, Neal and Petra were studying some film recordings that might be of use, as well as stocking up on food and clothing for everyone.

When the day finally came, Erin managed to sneak out of the house to be by herself. She wandered down to the beach, passing groups of holidaymakers beginning to pack up for the day. The sun sat low in the sky, hovering above wisps of cloud. It all looked so normal, none of these people would ever guess what was happening just a few miles away beneath the ground. Wondering what strangers would say if she told them what she now knew, Erin pulled off her canvas shoes and crept towards the water's edge.

She gasped when the icy coldness tickled her toes, the wavelet hissing away from her before curling back and covering her bare feet. It reminded her this was real. The wet sand beneath her feet was caving in from the pressure of the surge, leaving her perched on two tiny islands, precarious just like her life at this moment in time. Erin stared out across the Atlantic Ocean at a boat in the distance sailing along to who knows where. A memory came to her then. A paper boat being launched into the sea and the waves flooding it until it sank without trace. Tears of sadness at losing my little boat. The sweet taste of ice cream. Someone dabbing at my face with a tissue and smiling down at me. I can't see her face; her halo is too bright. My tears slowing as the ice melted in my mouth. Just forget, the angel had said. Just forget.

Erin had forgotten, but thoughts and memories are only just buried beneath the surface, and hazy images now came to her. She remembered the angel taking her hand and walking her to the edge of the world, their feet leaving prints in the sand. In her memories, Erin was running to the water giggling, kicking her bare legs at the waves. I must have been about three or four. Something or someone had made me sad, and it wasn't just losing the tiny paper boat. The image of that day became more solid for a brief moment before drifting away on the wind, and in her mind's eye, she saw Stella standing a few feet away watching her. All those years ago, she had run into her mummy's arms and cried and cried.

Now, standing in the same spot on the drenched sand, Erin knew she hadn't seen an angel all those years ago – it was the sun, not a halo, shining behind her. What did I have to forget? I must remember; it might be important. Mum will know. Mum! A sudden ache in her chest brought her thoughts to Stella. I miss her so much. They were limiting their contact with everyone apart from those involved. When Erin tried Stella, the phone kept going to voicemail. She thought of her mum back home in Newton and what her father had told her. "Mum's trying to help us but will carry on with the running of her shop. We must keep up appearances, not for the locals, but for the authorities." She was too busy to even talk to me. Does she really care about us?

Images of home came to her. What about Petra and her family? Are they keeping up appearances? Dad said Neal was contacted by Z11. Can we trust Neal? Petra finds him very irritating, and I think he's a slimeball, but surely, he's on our side. Remembering the lesson where she last saw Z11 brought more fears to mind. Something had changed with that contingent: their behaviour was very odd; their use of words was strange, and the teacher's reactions towards them frightened her.

Her thoughts now turned to her brother. Mal was growing stronger every day - he said he was determined to be there when the time came for action. Just like him, Erin mused, wiggling her toes in the sand. Earlier that day, finally looking like his old self again, he confided in her, his concern for Cara, which of course met with a derisory comment from Erin. She couldn't care less what had happened to his girlfriend.

"A penny for your thoughts." It was Pandora splashing towards her, sandals in one hand. "I thought I'd find you here."

"Is it time to go?" Erin asked, stepping away from the trickling waves, leaving two foot-shaped holes which were soon filled up by sand. Not leaving a trace, she thought. It looks like we've never been here. Inside in her heart, she locked away her own secrets, some of which she still didn't know the answer. She just had to find the key.

"Yes, I'm afraid it is."

They fell in step with each other as they trudged back to the bridge spanning the babbling river cleaving through the beach. The last few remnants of visitors were trailing away too. Children dragging spades through the sand; parents weighed down by deck chairs and overflowing bags; dogs barking, pulling on their leads to be set free. Once they were both on the bridge, Erin looked back to see another sailing boat bobbing on the sea, its triangular sails catching the wind and the bow cutting through silken ribbon waves. One day, I will come back, she vowed.

Pandora turned off the car engine, and Erin slumped down in the front seat. They were parked on a side road along from the farm, waiting with Miranda and Frankie for the signal to get going. Further up the road, Patrick and Mal were busy operating a drone to fly over the land above the underground school. It was set to drop canisters of sleeping-gas crystals down the air vents into Zephyr.

The idea of gassing people horrified Erin. What if they killed someone by accident? What if Edward doesn't get the breathing equipment in time? She chewed her fingernails until they were ragged. Thought Reform was set for 10th August for Febcon, and then all the other contingents would follow. She had implored Patrick to get everyone out, and he explained they couldn't - they didn't have the capacity to house over 100 children and they would need more time. We will get them out, he promised her, one day.

The Teardrops won't know what's hit them, she pondered, drawing tear shapes in the condensation forming on the car windows. Dusk was falling now, stealing away the sun and all the colour in the world. Frankie gazed at the phone screen Erin held in her hand. "20:55," he whispered to Miranda without taking his eyes from the numbers. "Thursday, 6th August. 12 and a white circle. What's that mean, Erin?"

Erin whispered back, "It's the temperature. The circle indicates night-time and a full moon."

"Isn't it amazing Z8, I mean Miranda?" To Erin, he sounded like a little boy on Christmas day. She smiled to herself. Wow, if he thinks this is fantastic, wait 'till he sees what else it can do.

Patrick had thought of everything. They wouldn't use their own phones – he had purchased two from a man in Castleton, and he had done something to them so they couldn't be tracked. Erin wasn't sure how or what he had done to it, but she was glad of his expertise. What she still wasn't sure about was Frankie.

How would he cope going back in? There had been yet another episode the previous night – Frankie had been kicking and screaming in his sleep – and two or three times before that he had been howling and rocking like a demented person. She reflected: he might be a danger to Miranda and me, once we are inside Zephyr. There was no going back now, though.

An eerie silence washed over the four people cocooned inside the little car. The digital numbers flicked to show 21:00, and an alarm beeped as Patrick's face appeared on the screen.

"Hi. We've dropped the crystals of sleeping gas down the air vents. They should be taking effect now. It's your turn guys. Edward will be by the main door to the Central Hub. He's cut off all alarms. We'll bring the minibus round to the front entrance while you're in there. You don't have long. You must be out by 23:00. Good luck."

"Okay, Dad. See you later." Erin took a deep breath and turning to the others, grinned. "Let's go!"

After sidling up the lane, with Pandora driving as slow as a hearse, Miranda, Erin and Frankie tumbled out and lifted thin metal air tanks to their backs. Strapping them on tightly, they set off along the path towards the farmhouse. By the door, they stopped and pulled on breathing masks, turning on the air valve. They each gave the okay sign and nodded. Erin was able to speak to the others, but for now, she remained silent, the enormity of what they were about to do playing on her mind.

The light above the front door helped them to see while Frankie broke a pane of glass, and gingerly extending his arm through the spiky frame, turned the lock on the other side. The door sprang open, and the three of them crept inside.

In the living room, just off the main hallway, the farmer and his wife were cuddled up in front of the television set, fast asleep with a documentary on lion cubs displayed on the large flat screen. Their dog lay on its back, paws in the air snoring, its back leg occasionally twitching as it ran through dreamy fields. Frankie closed the door to the room and blocked up any gaps by squirting a quick-drying foam into the keyhole and between the door and its frame. "They'll sleep like babies," Frankie smirked.

Erin led the way to the lift entrance and punched the button; the doors opening immediately. Once inside the glass box, all three of them gasped when the lift descended into the Central Hub. They had all been in there before but to see it from this height showed what a beautiful oasis it was. The water rushed over high rocks and gushed down into a sparkling blue pool. The plethora of verdant plants with huge leaves of emerald, olive and lime green made Pandora's garden fade in comparison. Gentle music accompanied the splash of water. Visitors would see it as being a tranquil place. Now, two beige bodies sprawled across the floor made it look more like a murder scene.

Leaving the glass lift, the three young people dodged around the sleeping bodies and hurried across to the large white door leading to the main corridors of Zephyr. Once there, Erin pressed the button, and the door slid open to reveal bodies lining the walls, some in grey, others in blue and most in white. Some were slumped in a seated position; others curled up like a foetus and most sprawled across the floor, their arms and legs stretched out.

Edward should be here with the Teardrops. Where were they? Erin swallowed hard and beckoned to the others. She gave quick instructions of what they should do, and they separated. Miranda stayed with Frankie and wandered down the corridor towards the Nourishment Sector. Erin turned the opposite way to the Correction Sector and set off, pausing every so often to check rooms. Bodies were scattered everywhere, the bright colours of the various teachers standing out against the detritus of grey and white.

It was as silent as a mortuary and Erin's breath quickened as she searched for signs of Edward and the Teardrops. Studying the faces of the fallen, she realised she didn't know what all the students, due to escape, even looked like. "I knew this wasn't a good idea. They haven't got the breathing equipment in time. What a disaster!" she whispered aloud. "I'm going to need Frankie and Miranda."

Deciding to continue for now in the hope Edward would appear, Erin trudged on, her breathing echoing in her ears. Rounding a corner, a large sign indicated the Correction Sector. Erin's hands trembled standing by the door, awful memories of this place filtering into her mind. The doors swung back and there - wearing a brown uniform and a mask making his eyes bulge like a dead fish - was Edward.

TREFOIL HQ

Transcript from meeting

John Johnson: I am not happy with Dorling at all.
She may well compromise NN2000.

Joyce Williams: I agree, but we don't have anyone who
can take her place at short notice.

Oliver Irons: She has had some success with her methods
and has given us interesting information on how the mind
works. Her research will help us with our plans.

Joyce Williams: What about the rest of the staff in
Zephyr? Can they be trusted? Perhaps there should be a
lockdown for a short period of time?

Oliver Irons: We will monitor for the next few days and
then reassess.

Chapter 9

 Miranda and Frankie plodded on along the corridors, stepping over bodies being careful not to tread on anyone. At the Nourishment Sector, the room was empty apart from two Orderlies who had fallen asleep at the counter where food was usually dished out.

Soft music played from speakers surreptitiously hidden, while black smoke curled out from the kitchen beyond and Frankie hurried to check it out. He returned brandishing a blackened burnt out pan and Miranda could see him beaming inside his mask. She waved at him and pointed to the door. He nodded, dropped the pan with a clatter and then followed her out.

Continuing along deserted corridors, making their way towards the Nod Pods, it was eerily quiet. Miranda, her breath loud in her ears, climbed one of the ladders to check inside the pods and soon discovered they were empty. Classroom after classroom was checked, some with sleeping bodies hunched over desks and computer screens. Miranda pulled up her sleeve and peered at the watch she had been given – 21:45 - there was still time.

There was no sign of Edward or any of the Teardrops and Frankie called to her.

"Let's go back. Hopefully, Erin's found them."

Miranda nodded and turned to go, but as she did so, she caught sight of a girl lying prone on the floor of one of the Learning Labs. She was the image of Petra. Horrified, she ran after Frankie and grabbed his arm. Turning towards her, his eyes suddenly flashed with anger, and he struck her hard across the face, dislodging the breathing mask. He shoved her away before running off down the corridor. She swayed for a moment and then like a tower of children's bricks she toppled over, banging her head hard against the wall.

Then everything went black.

Miranda woke to find Frankie holding her tightly to his chest as he carried her, her shallow breathing growing stronger with every step. Struggling in his grip, she frantically tried to escape from his clutches. He was much stronger than her and Miranda was feeling sick and woozy. It must be the gas, she thought. Her mind was playing tricks with her. Questions tumbled around her head, and strange answers twisted their way into her thoughts. Where's he taking me? What if he's on their side? Is he going to kill me? I should never have trusted him. This is all my fault. An image of a girl looking like death wormed its way through the shadowy depths of her subconscious. Z63 - I must get back to Z63. Miranda began to kick, but Frankie pulled her even closer.

Arriving back at the area by the door to the Central Hub, it was just like before with bodies littering the place. Frankie stopped and kneeling, he lay Miranda gently on the floor. Cowering, afraid of another attack, she tried to pull away, but he was too quick for her and grabbing her by both shoulders he looked into her eyes.

"I'm so sorry. Have I hurt you? Please forgive me."

Miranda glared at him. "Why did you do that? How can I trust you now?" Breathing hard, she wrenched from his grip, dragging herself away and finally sagging against a wall.

Frankie sat back on his heels, opening his arms out wide. "It's this place. Zephyr has created me to not feel emotions, to not trust anyone, to fight when cornered." His hands fell, and his head drooped. "When I'm with you, though, I feel something here." Frankie pressed his hand against his breastbone. "Please help me." He stretched his arm towards her, fingers like a star.

Miranda sighed and reached out until the tips of her fingers touched his. That connection was all she needed to trust in Frankie. She understood – they were both creations of Zephyr and of Trefoil, and as a unit, they could change lives, not only their own but all the others who were held there. Then, shuffling forwards on her bottom, she wrapped her arms around him, feeling his warmth and strength flow through her.

"We must go back for Z63. That's why I grabbed you," she explained when they finally let go of each other.

"I'll go. You need to rest. Where was she?"

"In Learning Lab 3, I think."

"I'll be right back," Frankie said, staggering to his feet and jogging off down the corridor.

Miranda looked about her. Where was Erin? She should be back by now. I hope she's found Edward. Feeling dizzy again, she closed her eyes for a minute or two and then gingerly held her head feeling for bumps and cuts.

What was that? A noise of what sounded like feet tramping hard on the ground alarmed her.

Quickly, she lay down, behind the other students, using their prone bodies to hide her while keeping an eye on the corridor beyond.

The footsteps echoed, getting closer and closer.

Edward was standing alone in the Correction Sector. He took Erin by the hand and led her to the cells. She wasn't sure what she would find and remembered Pandora's ironic comment of being careful opening things. Peering through the glass in each of the doors, she saw a person in grey sitting on a hard bed wearing breathing apparatus.

Turning to Edward, Erin asked, "What's going on? Why have you locked them up?"

"It was the best way of getting the breathing apparatus to them, but I can't open the cell doors now." To support this, he pointed a remote control at the locked doors. Nothing. "It might be because I disconnected the alarms. I think I've messed up."

Erin gasped. "We're running out of time. Have you checked the batteries?"

The skeletal Orderly looked back and pulled a sour face. "Of course, I have. I'm not stupid – I don't care what they say about me. I do have a brain."

Erin raised her eyebrows at this admission and apologised before adding, "Where are the spare remotes stored?"

"Back in the Central Hub."

"We'll both go," she said, pulling him by the arm. "They'll be fine here." She nodded towards the cells before checking her watch. There was over an hour left before the sleeping gas wore off.

Racing back, their boots thudding hard on the floor, the two covered the distance quickly. While Edward crept into the Central Hub, Erin stood, feet apart surveying the scene. All the people around her looked peaceful, they didn't look like they were in pain for which she was thankful, and she began to relax a little.

A sudden movement in her peripheral vision pulled tension back into her muscles, and she turned in slow motion to see more clearly. Holding her breath, she steeled herself for an attack. A young man dressed in white was lying on his side, and as she watched, his arm lying along his bent leg, slid to the floor; the movement causing him to snuffle and grunt. Erin prepared herself, clenching both fists and holding them in front of her chest, the right hand behind the left, sliding her right foot back into a lunge. She took a deep breath and exhaled, relaxing her muscles but ready to defend herself.

The boy's eyes flickered, his shoulder wavered, a signal perhaps the drug was wearing off. Erin held her position, slate-grey eyes vigilant as his whole body slumped over into a prone position, his drug-induced sleep reinforced by a snort.

Erin flinched, but remained in position: behind the boy was a figure struggling to stand. It reached out to her before collapsing back down in a small pathetic heap. "Erin…" The voice was hesitant and full of pain, and it took a few seconds for Erin to register the person was adorned with breathing apparatus.

"Miranda… oh no, what's happened to you?" she cried, rushing to her sister's side. Erin was horrified to see a deep gash in the girl's forehead, oozing blood and the skin of her cheek turning into a purple-red bruise.

Miranda struggled to sit up, and Erin helped her by holding her close. Miranda gave a weak smile. "It was Frankie…"

"I knew we shouldn't have trusted him. Where is he? Has he just abandoned you?"

Miranda shook her head. A tremor washed over her, and she collapsed back onto the floor.

"No! Please, no!" Erin screamed.

Edward came running, brandishing a remote in each hand. "What the….?"

"It was Frankie!" she shouted, hugging Miranda to her chest and then swaying like a mother rocks a child to sleep.

Edward took charge. "Erin, come on, help me. She's just fainted." He helped Miranda to a sitting position and then gently held her head between her knees until a coughing and spluttering told them both she was back from the land of nod. After a few minutes, they managed to get her to stand, and between them, they dragged her to the lift and placed her down against the glass.

Edward ran off to the cells while Erin watched over her sister. What a mess, she thought. When is it all going to end?

A shout from the entrance of the Central Hub summoned her back from her thoughts. Turning to welcome Edward and the Teardrops, she was shocked to see Frankie stumbling towards her, the body of a girl in his arms.

"You!" Erin shouted. "What did you do to my sister? You monster!" She ran at him pummelling his head, his arms, his shoulders, causing him to loosen his grip and the girl almost fell to the floor. Frankie heaved his heavy load back to his chest and then using his back to shield himself and the sleeping girl, he staggered to carefully lay her down next to Miranda.

Dodging Erin's flying fists, Frankie managed to take her by the arms and pinning them to her sides, said, "It was an accident. I didn't mean to do it. I would never do anything to hurt Z89."

Erin writhed in his grip, "You Mallory's are all the same. You're not a true Teardrop; you're a fake!" She stamped hard on Frankie's right foot and ducked down fast out of the circle of his arms. When he turned around, she was there aiming a roundhouse kick at his head. He shifted to one side, but she caught his shoulder. His eyes blazed, and he stepped back in a lunge to prepare to attack. Erin was ready for his punch and blocked it, following it with a fast punch of her own, but Frankie raised his arm and stopped it in mid-flow. Spinning round, Erin aimed a back kick to Frankie's chest winding him. He stood back coughing into his mask, bent over catching his breath and then prepared once again to attack.

"STOP!"

115

A shout from behind them rent the air, and they froze. Edward stood in the doorway to the Central Hub, a caterpillar of people trailing behind him. He was holding his hands high in the air, the palms flat towards them. Erin looked at Frankie, and he returned her stare. For a moment, the air around them was charged with electricity, sun shone down on them from the faraway ceiling, dust motes danced in the light.

"Erin..." A small voice came from Miranda. "Please... don't. It's not Frankie's fault. Blame Zephyr and Trefoil, but don't blame him."

"We mustn't fight between ourselves. If we do, then they have won," added Edward, herding his flock of students towards the lift doors.

"I went to find Z63," Frankie announced, stumbling over to the two girls. Erin stared at the little tableau and realised the sleeping girl next to Miranda was Petra's twin.

"I'm sorry," Erin blurted out, still not sure if she really meant it. Knowing they had to work together, for now, she raised her arms in submission.

"Me too," said Frankie, mirroring her action.

"Come on; we must get moving." Edward took charge, separating the group into two huddles. "We can't all go up at the same time. Frankie, carry Z63 please and Miranda, you must go too. Erin and I will come up with the remaining Teardrops."

Erin watched as they all trooped into the glass box, which then rose up towards the ceiling. "Edward, there's something I must do. We need the documents," she said, checking her watch. There still a little time before the gas wore off. "Give me a remote."

"Be quick!" Edward urged her, placing one into her outstretched hand.

Erin strode across to a large wooden door adorned with a pattern of squares and circles and pointed the remote towards it. The door swung open, to reveal the Principal's desk, immaculate as always. There was no sign of Miss Dorling, and Erin hurried round to the other side of the desk. She remembered files had been hidden in a cabinet behind a wall, but where was the button that activated this? Checking all the drawers and sliding her fingers under the rim of the table, Erin tried not to panic. Where was it? She tried to picture where Miss Dorling had been standing when the wall had closed. That's right; she stood over here. Erin moved to her left. Miss Dorling used her left hand. Erin stretched out her own left hand. A tiny flicker of blue light scanned her fingers; there was no button. It was read by a fingerprint. Erin breathed out hard, biting her lip.

"Hurry up!" Edward hissed from outside the door. "The lift is back; we must go."

Erin ignored him and began to pace up and down, thinking about what to do. A door hidden at the back of the office slid open to reveal another room. Stepping across the threshold, Erin let out a gasp, the space surrounding her was beautiful and everything a different shade of purple. Mauve cushions lay on a dark purple couch; lilac walls showed off light fittings dripping with lavender crystals twinkling in the light that cascaded down from an ornate ceiling chandelier. The bed linen was plum coloured silk, piled high with cushions of purple sequins, purple fur and purple satin.

And there laid on this magnificent bed was Miss Dorling's sleeping form, her fingers dangling over the side, razor-sharp nails swathed in amethyst nail gel. Erin took a step closer, and then another few steps until she could see the rise and fall of the woman's chest. An idea came to her, except to accomplish it, she would need help.

Turning on her heel, Erin strode off back into the main office and out to the Central Hub. "Come on; we must go." It was Edward shouting to her from the open lift.

"Let them go up. I need you to help me in here," Erin answered nodding at the doorway.

"We only have a few minutes. Come on!" Edward started waving his arms at her as though the gesture would speed her up. Erin was determined though; she knew they needed documentation to find out more about Zephyr and Trefoil. Going across to him, Erin stayed his arm and looked deep into his eyes.

"Please. We must do this. I can't do this without you." Erin began to pull him away from the lift.

"Let me just get this lot on their way." Edward indicated the grey mass of people peering at her through the glass. After pressing some buttons, he slid his gangly frame out of the box, the doors closed, and the lift ascended.

Once they were in the office, Erin showed him what she wanted to do. "You're mad!" he exclaimed.

"It's the only way."

"Okay, let's give it a go."

Erin wheeled an office chair through to the bedroom and then parked it next to the bed. Edward pulled the bedcovers towards him, the inert figure moving with them. Lifting her over his shoulder, he held her while Erin wheeled the chair under the body. Then together they laid her down onto the seat. Edward suddenly grinned, his whole face lighting up. "This is fun." Erin didn't smile back. I will never understand this man – he has a weird idea of what incorporates fun.

The two pulled and pushed the chair towards the desk in the office, where, with Edward holding the dead weight of Miss Dorling upright, Erin grabbed the woman's hand and passed it under the sensor on the desk.

A blue flash, then nothing. Erin held her breath, willing it to work. She counted to ten and then when she was beginning to think it wasn't going to work the light glowed purple, and the wall to their left slid open.

Erin and Edward looked at each other. She nodded at him before making her way to the cabinet that was jammed in tightly. There were hundreds of files, locked behind glass doors. "We need a key." Erin's shoulders sagged. They were beaten.

"Key coming through," shouted Edward, barging past her. "Stand aside." He was wielding a hammer which he used to smash the lock and then just for good measure; he crashed it hard against the glass. Splinters, as sharp as daggers fired out in all directions and Erin instinctively threw herself to the floor in front of the desk, covering her head with her arms.

"As I said, this is fun," he laughed, pulling open the doors to the wrecked cabinet. Dropping the hammer, he grabbed armloads of files and disappeared out through the main door. "Come on, Erin."

Erin shook herself, dazed for a moment with shock. Glass icicles lay all around. The air seemed to swirl in the wake of a tornado. Clambering to her feet, she stumbled to the cabinet and heaved a pile of folders towards her. Hugging them close to her chest, she headed for the door. Her eye was caught by a shimmer; the Trefoil symbol shining in the dim light, adorning a metal box file.

Erin bent to pick it up, trying not to drop her haul. Behind her, came a sigh and a cough. Spinning round, prepared to see Miss Dorling there behind her alive and kicking, she was surprised to see the woman still slumped in the chair. Erin breathed deeply. In her haste to protect herself, first one, then another cardboard document slipped from her arms. The trickle became a torrent, an avalanche in full flow. Before she knew what was happening, she was surrounded by the details of all the students in Zephyr, reams of paper had escaped, unlike the students, to end up as a mass of white snow piled up around her ankles.

I need to get moving, she thought. Erin knelt and pulled cardboard and paper towards her, gathering it into some sort of order. She froze, no sound this time to disturb her. A piece of paper she held in her hand was covered in words, and at the bottom, a red ink stain was growing like a fungus, becoming larger as she stared. Looking across at the sleeping woman, Erin was aware she also had red ink peppering her arms and face. No, not ink...blood.

The glass missiles had embedded themselves into the Principal's skin. Just like tears falling, blood was dripping down her cheeks. Erin had felt only hatred for her, yet now she felt compassion for another human being. Laying the folders down, she staggered across and listened. There was a shallow breath, and the chest was rising and falling. Erin took the end of a purple scarf, laying around the neck, and dabbed at the cuts on the face.

The air around the two people settled. Erin focusing on wiping away blood wasn't ready.

The eyes sprang open, and Erin found her own grey eyes staring straight into the violet ones of Esme Dorling.

Report: 2467

To: John Johnson, Joyce Williams, Oliver Irons

From: Esme Dorling

- We are in LOCKDOWN after being attacked by gas.

- Several students, from various contingents, have escaped.

- We are currently assessing the damage caused and listing the escapees.

- I am being attended by a doctor due to multiple lacerations from broken glass.

- The Winslow family are to blame for this, and we request your help in finding the perpetrators.

- We are delaying Thought Reform until the school is back to normal.

Chapter 10

Miranda was back on the surface and breathing in fresh air; her head clearing. She aided the others with their breathing apparatus, and then along with Frankie tried to guide them onto the minibus. The students were staring up at the ghostly-white full moon suspended above them. One of them, a small girl with bright eyes, even reached out to touch it. "Is it real?" she asked. Miranda nodded, remembering the first time she had seen the real moon on leaving Zephyr.

"Oh, yes," she breathed. "It's beautiful, isn't it?"

"Yes. The Sea of Serenity, the Sea of Tranquillity and the Sea of Nectar are all on the moon," the girl answered. "Such beautiful names."

"There's also the Sea of Crises," responded Frankie. "And there will be a crisis if you don't get moving." His face showed no emotion as he herded the young people like cattle to the open doors of the vehicle before them.

"Where's Erin and Edward? They should be back by now," Patrick called from inside the farmhouse, where he was pacing back and forth.

Miranda ran to him in the shadowy depths. Behind the glass of the closed door leading to the living room, the farmer and his wife were still fast asleep on the sofa, the television now showing a late-night movie – a car chase, with police cars piling up on top of each other – and the farm dog was now laid flat out on the floor, snoring.

"They'll be up in a minute, I'm sure," she said, and at that moment the lift appeared, full of people. The grey figures stepped out, agape with fear. "It's okay," Miranda said to them. "Keep your masks on until you leave the building." She guided them towards Mal and Pandora, who were waiting to remove masks.

"Where is she?" shouted Patrick as the figures trailed away.

Miranda came running back.

"I can't lose her again." Patrick strode into the yawning mouth of the lift. "I'm going to get her."

"But the gas will be wearing off soon." Frankie had now appeared in the house. "It's madness to go down there."

"I don't care; she's my daughter. I have to try!"

"Then, I'm coming with you. I know the place better than you." Frankie hurried after Patrick.

"Wait, I know where she'll be," called Miranda.

Patrick pressed the button on the lift to hold the doors open, his eyes narrowing behind his mask.

"We both agreed we'd go to the Principal's office to get files on the students. Look there first."

Patrick nodded, letting his hand drop and the doors closed.

Miranda paused for a moment before returning to the cold night air. A sea of sad faces stared out from the minibus. She knew she had to talk to them – to reassure them. Peeping through the open doorway, she said, "Once Erin...Z84 is back, we'll be going. Please fasten your seat belts; we have a long journey ahead of us." She glanced at Z63's sleeping form (the effects of the gas were still in her system) and tenderly tucked the seat belt around her, clicking it into place.

"Z63's family have rented a house in Shropshire; that's where we will be staying."

A boy, sitting at the back of the minibus, raised his hand. "Excuse me. May I speak?"

"Of course, Z19 Maycon."

"Teardrops," he said, and everyone turned towards him. He raised both hands, so they were level with his eyes. In one slow movement, he curved his fingers to create the teardrop shape. "We have shed many tears and will shed many more. This is the next chapter for us all. This is what we have been fighting for. Trefoil must not win. Our metamorphosis will not be of their making – we will decide our own future. We are the future. Together, we will fight to stop Zephyr." Z19 brought his hands to touch and created a butterfly.

In silence, they all copied him until the air was a kaleidoscope of butterflies.

Erin froze – the iridescent irises before her held no life. The eyelids lowered.

Like an alarm screaming in her head, her unconscious was warning her to leave. Now!

Scooping up the pile of folders, ensuring she had the metal one embossed with the Trefoil symbol, Erin stumbled to the open door. It was barred by a solid figure of a man. Looking up, desperate to escape and to take her treasure with her, she saw it was Frankie.

Erin stepped back, hugging the folders to her, scared he might attack her. "It's all right," he said. "Please. Let me help."

Gritting her teeth, she handed him everything, except the Trefoil folder. Still not sure whether to trust him or not, Erin was desperate to look after this one.

"STOP!"

The sickly voice came from close behind her, cutting through the air. Erin whipped round. Esme Dorling was standing, her face turning purple with rage, blood trickling from the copious cuts covering her skin.

"Come back here!" Miss Dorling ordered, her voice dripping with hatred.

Erin felt strong arms surround her from behind. Twisting her head, ready to strike her attacker, her field of vision revealed a familiar figure. Completing the turn fully, she fell into his arms, and he held her tightly.

"I'm here, lovely girl," Patrick whispered. The two of them faced the purple vision before them.

"Erin will not come back, nor will Miranda. We will fight you and your Trefoil wolves, whoever they are, and get justice for all our children." Patrick's strident voice echoed around the Hub. When he slammed the huge oak door shut, the sound reverberated, entwining with the echo. The two beige Administrators, still on the floor, were shaking themselves into wakefulness as a screeching alarm tore around the Hub.

"Time to go!" Patrick shouted, and they ran to the waiting lift where Frankie stood, his arms hugging the stories of the children of Zephyr.

"Mum? Hi, it's me. Look, I'm sorry for everything I did." Erin paused, her breath steaming up the screen of the mobile. She'd always hated speaking to an answering machine. "Mum, please pick up..." An empty silence stretched out, across the miles. "Love you."

"She's still not answering," Erin explained to Patrick, handing him the phone. They had pulled into a truck-stop, just off the main road. Sheltering in the dark side of a massive beast of a lorry - the August night casting a chill - father and daughter stood close, their shadows merging into one.

"Don't worry. We'll try again in the morning... on the landline. No mobiles from now on." With that, Patrick strode up to the cab and passed several phones to the driver. "Thanks, mate. We really appreciate you doing this."

The door of the cab slammed in answer, and the lorry's engine roared into life.

"He's driving across to Kent to get the tunnel to France. He'll offload the phones at various places on the way. It should help to confuse anyone trying to track us." Erin nodded and strolled back to the minibus, hitching up the metal folder hiding inside her jacket, its top edge digging into her collar bone.

"Do you think Pandora and Edward will be safe in Cornwall?" Erin asked.

"We need them there to keep us informed of what's going on. They'll be fine. Edward's going to lay low at Pandora's."

"Edward acted very strangely back there. He went crazy."

"Probably, from all the pain and frustration he's felt all these years working in that prison."

Erin climbed into the front seat of the minibus, next to Mal, who asked her sleepily how their mum was.

Patrick turned on the engine and manoeuvred out onto the road where the red lights of distant cars glowed in the darkness.

"She didn't answer."

"You know Mum and phones. Anyway, it's late; she's probably gone to bed." Mal sighed.

Erin nodded, leaning her head on Mal's shoulder.

They raced along motorways, swept through towns and villages and navigated narrow country lanes. Finally, after travelling under the cover of darkness, guided by a silver moon, they arrived at a large, sprawling, brick-built house. It was 3am.

Everyone was exhausted. Neal and Bianca, Petra's parents, guided them to various rooms where they could sleep. Some were on old rickety camp-beds, others on inflatable mattresses, some slept on beanbags or a sofa, and some were lucky to have a proper bed. Lights were extinguished, and the silence of the Shropshire countryside washed over them. High above the house, the moon bobbed like a paper boat on an ocean of cobalt ink. Erin, lying on a sofa in the conservatory, wrapped in a sleeping bag, watched the clouds hug the silent orb; her mind full of moments from the last day or two. Frankie... Miss Dorling... Edward... it was like counting sheep, and she finally gave in and slept.

Breakfast was a noisy affair with the Teardrops finding their voices and savouring not only the food on offer but the chance to speak freely. Erin and Miranda sat watching from the side-lines, nudging each other when someone did or said something funny or interesting.

Suddenly, Erin grasped her sister's hand tightening her grip. "You're hurting me. What's the matter, Erin?"

"It's Petra," Erin said under her breath, her eyes following the girl who had entered the room. She's cut her hair short. I wonder why? Another girl followed her in - this one displaying a head of golden stubble like a cornfield in harvest time - Z63. Petra was trying to mimic her twin.

"Oh, how lovely, they've found each other. Let's go and see them." Miranda braced herself to stand, but Erin pulled her back.

"No."

"Why not? Petra's your friend. And she's mine now, too."

"It's complicated. I can't..." Erin stopped. Shay, dreadlocks swinging, shoulders hunched, was trailing the two girls into the room. The last time she had seen him was at the Seven Spirits when she had realised her friend had betrayed her. The three of them were welcomed by Bianca, and they helped themselves to food and drinks. Erin crumbled, letting go of Miranda's hand, casting her eyes down, she fell back against the seat cushions trying to hide from view.

What's he doing here? How could Petra do this to me? Questions swirled around in Erin's head matching the churning of her stomach. Feeling as though she was being watched, Erin glanced up to find Shay's rich brown eyes burning into hers, his mouth upturned in an enigmatic smile. Then to her consternation, he winked at her. Erin sneered, turning her back and raised her coffee to her lips. How dare he make fun of me? She thought.

The sound of hands clapping together caused Erin to peep over her mug. It was Petra's mum. "Everyone, can I have your attention please?" She spoke with a slight accent; Erin knew Bianca had been brought up in Shropshire, but her voice was a mixture of places – a touch of the north, a sprinkling of Scottish borrowed from Neal and a dash of Midlands twang. While she stood, waiting for silence, her demeanour showed she was used to public speaking and to being in control. The chatter of voices diminished to a whisper, and then a hush descended. The twelve Teardrops, still in their grey uniforms; along with the adults and the other young people, turned their faces towards Bianca.

Being slight in stature, she was standing on a chair so they could see her. However, being dressed in white jeans and a bubble-gum pink top, emblazoned with a giant gold star, you couldn't miss her. Bianca's hair was blonde like that of her daughters, but hers was long and wavy, and as always, her make-up was flawless.

She began with a loud, confident voice. "You can all have a shower – there are plenty of towels. There's another shower by the swimming pool as well as those upstairs and the one on this floor. We have toothbrushes for you all and toiletries and hair..." Bianca paused. Several pairs of eyes stared her down. The shaved heads of the Teardrops and her own daughter were spread out around the room like pebbles on a beach, some fuzzy with new hair growth. Her voice began to waver. "Sorry, I didn't think. Erm... what else... oh yes. We have clothes and shoes for you all. I'm sorry they're not overly exciting – it was the best we could do in a short time."

Bianca continued, getting back into her stride. "Can you meet in the living room at 11:30 so we can explain our plans. Please be patient with us. This is all new for us too. Just remember you're safe here; Trefoil knows nothing of this house. We are mobile phone free, so they shouldn't be able to track us."

Patrick added with a grin, "Hopefully, they'll be following several lorries all over the country."

"Come and collect some clothes. Don't forget, you are safe, and you are loved." Bianca finished and went to climb off her makeshift podium. Just like a switch clicking on, all the Zephyr students including Miranda and Frankie stood and in one voice intoned, "We are one being. We belong here. We are loved."

Bianca blinked hard, her eyes flicking from one figure to another. "What have I done?" she breathed.

"Don't worry, Bee," Patrick said, offering his hand to help her down. "It's something they do in Zephyr."

The sea of faces became still, smiles returned, and then each of the Teardrops filed out of the room, collecting clothing as they went.

"We have a lot of work to do," sighed Patrick. "These kids have been indoctrinated all their lives; we must be gentle and patient. We'll get there, but first coffee." He held his mug out to Bianca.

MESSAGE

To: Trefoil

From: Orderly O5 and O7

We followed the lorry as requested. Registration number G55EBY.

They made several stops before Dover. We contacted the Kent police informing them of dangerous driving by this lorry driver, and he was stopped at the Ferry terminal.

Further lorries were followed into France and similarly stopped by French police. No one from Zephyr has been found.

Mobile phones were discovered to have a tracking device fitted to them. This was not fitted by Trefoil. We await instructions.

Chapter 11

Miranda perched herself on the edge of a suede-covered sofa, while everyone filed into the living room. She took a moment to take in the plush surroundings. They had come a long way from Zephyr, both literally and metaphorically. A large gilt mirror above the stone fireplace reflected the bright colours as the Teardrops took their seats, some sitting on the floor. One girl stroked the dense cream carpet and patterned rug while another held a cushion to her cheek, both savouring the softness, the luxuriousness they had never known.

Through the windows, Miranda could see trees, shrubs, flowers all bathing in the morning sunshine and beyond the garden, fields of golden wheat waving gently in the breeze.

"Good morning to you all and welcome," Patrick said, standing in front of the fireplace. "Are we all here?" He frowned as Frankie sidled in late and took his place by the door.

"All here," he said, crossing his arms and leaning against the doorframe.

"Good. Then we can get started." Patrick breathed in deeply before continuing. "There are many things we need to tell you, some of which can wait until another time, but I want to be absolutely clear from the start, you can trust everyone here."

Miranda looked around at the host of people crammed into the living room; their eyes fixated on Patrick as he spoke. "We need to be honest and support each other because it won't be easy. You have spent your whole lives in Zephyr and are all very highly educated and intelligent young people, but..." he trailed off at this point. "Things have happened to some of you in there, that will affect how you behave in the outside world. You will find it incredibly difficult to socialise, to communicate, to sleep. You will be disorientated and, as Stella, my wife would say, discombobulated."

"You will discover things about yourselves and your families that might be upsetting." At the word, families, the Teardrops began to look around in surprise.

"We don't have families." It was Z73 who had spoken. A slim young man with olive skin unblemished apart from an L shaped scar. With a husky voice, he continued. "You tell us of this, but we have always been told we were removed from the woman who bore us so we can be individuals. Where is the evidence of this?"

The silence following his question floated on the air. Speckles of dust danced in the sunbeams stretching through the windows. The gentle tick-tock of a grandfather clock marked the passing of time.

"I am the evidence of this," Miranda announced jumping up and going across to Patrick. A ripple of gasps ruffled the air. "This is... my father." She smiled at him and the grin he returned lit up his whole face.

"Yes, this is my daughter." He hugged her tightly. "Erin?"

"I'm here, Dad." Erin came to join them and wrapped her arms around them both.

They stepped apart and stood in a line facing the room. "Erin and Miranda are my twin daughters, and to my eternal shame, I gave Miranda away when she was a baby. I will do everything in my power to keep them out of Zephyr. I will do everything I can to find your families and to find out the truth behind Zephyr and Trefoil."

Miranda was unaware of the effect this announcement was having on the Teardrops until she turned and faced them all. She looked from one to the other, a few of them were smiling, two had tears cascading down their cheeks, and several looked stunned, their eyes like deep chasms. Then the voices began to babble. Words were tossed around the room like boats in a storm. Accusations were thrown like gravel pulled by a riptide on a beach.

Petra spoke above the maelstrom of voices, her words piercing through the darkness of confusion; a beam of light guiding them all back to safety. "Please, you must believe Patrick. He, just like my parents, didn't know what was going to happen to us. I never knew I had a twin sister until my best friend, Erin told me." She looked across at Erin, whose eyes were narrowing at this confession. "I didn't believe her. Why would my parents lie to me all these years? But they didn't really lie; they just kept the truth hidden for all our sakes. They thought they were doing the best for their families." Petra stopped abruptly. "Erin, I'm so sorry for not trusting you. Please can we be friends again? I miss you so much."

Erin lifted her head, her eyes steely, her hands curling into fists. "No, Petra, I won't be your friend until you start telling me the truth!" she shouted and stormed out of the room. Petra glanced around her in shock at this anger and then hurried after Erin.

Miranda went to follow her, but Patrick held her arm and shook his head. "Leave them. They need to talk."

Patrick went on, "Okay, everyone, let's just sit down, and I'll endeavour to tell you our plans. You, of course, can chip in your ideas too."

Miranda returned to her perch and listened, marvelling at what had happened so far.

"We're going to sort through the files we managed to bring out of Zephyr. These will give us more background information about you all. We would like to contact your families and let them know you're all okay. Frankie, can you read out all the names from your list please?"

The Teardrops all answered in turn to their number and Contingent name. It was at that point, Neal, who had been quiet for most of the time, spoke up, his voice soft. "What about Z11? I've been communicating with him through the internet. Why's he not here?"

"Because he's not one of us." Frankie's answer was sharp. His stony tone continued. "I haven't had a chance to speak with you. Z11 is a Jancon; he's undergone Thought Reform. He's begun his Metamorphosis."

At that moment, the grandfather clock chimed the hour. Miranda held her breath and counted in her head. Twelve o'clock. The enormity of what Frankie and Neal were saying slowly seeped into her brain.

Neal slumped down, cradling his head between his hands, his sandy hair curling around his fingers. "This cannot be happening. I've put you all in danger." His Scottish ancestry breaking through his speech as he became more and more upset.

"Not necessarily," said Frankie. "Once I have a look at your messages to him, we might be able to use it to our advantage. We could do a double bluff."

Patrick nodded. "Don't worry, Neal. Okay, everyone. You have the rest of the day to yourselves. Please don't leave the grounds; you are welcome to wander around the garden. There's a games room and several TVs too. Lunch will be at one in the garden room. See you later."

The gathering broke up, with the Teardrops going off in twos and threes. Neal remained grief-stricken until Miranda came and stood in front of him. "Come on, let's go and have a look at those messages." His face brightened as he stood and allowed her and Frankie to lead him along to the dining room.

"Go away!" shouted Erin, stumbling towards the front door. Pulling it open, she flew down the stone steps towards a patch of lawn and a wooden bench, where she threw herself down, digging her heels into the mossy ground.

"No, I won't!" Petra retorted, following Erin to the bench. "I've had enough of this. I've apologised. We need to sort this out, once and for all." The girl stopped and faced Erin, hands on hips, legs astride, her eyes blazing.

"Go and talk to your boyfriend," Erin said. "He'll look after you." She folded her arms as a barrier between them.

"My boyfriend?"

"Yes. I know what you've been up to behind my back."

"What? Are you serious? I don't even have a boyfriend!"

"Shay. The handsome, gorgeous Shay." Erin spat the words out.

Petra just gaped at her. Then, closing her mouth, a twinkle came to her eyes, the corners of her mouth curled upwards, and a laugh exploded from her.

Suddenly, she was doubled up with laughter, tears flowing.

Erin was full of rage. "How dare you laugh at me? I saw you together at The Seven Spirits. He's here now… as part of the family!" She leapt from the bench and ran down the twisting driveway towards the road.

"Erin, come back! You don't understand." Petra was running after her now, the laughter dissolving on the wind.

At the electric gates, Erin grabbed the bars and rattled them hard. *Another prison: I can't take much more.* She turned as she heard Petra call her name again. "You've no idea what I've been through. I was locked up in that hellhole, knowing my best friend betrayed me."

"I would never betray you, Erin. Shay isn't my boyfriend. He's my cousin."

It was Erin's turn to gape. "You're joking, right?"

"No, I'm serious; he's definitely my cousin. I thought you understood that. You said you heard everything we said at the Seven Spirits. Is this why you won't be friends with me?" Petra was now standing before Erin, her eyes pleading with her.

"I saw you cuddling him and saying how you had found each other. I didn't wait to hear any more. I ran away after that." Tears began to course down Erin's face. "I'm sorry. I'm so sorry."

Erin felt Petra encircle her in a hug, and she sobbed into her friend's shoulder.

"I've missed you, Erin."

"I've missed you, too."

"I haven't missed the tears though and the soggy shoulders," Petra said, pulling away, squeezing the fabric of her T-shirt. Erin laughed, and Petra joined in.

"But I still don't see how he can be your cousin. He's been in our class for a year or two now – why didn't you know?"

They strolled back to the garden bench, arm in arm. Once they were seated, Petra began her tale. "Mum's brother was working in Nigeria; she lost contact with him through a family argument, many years ago. He married Shay's mum while he was out there, but when the marriage broke up, Shay was sent to England to live with her family, an aunt of his mum's. He took his mum's surname, Kalu. They wanted him to be educated in the UK."

Erin listened, sitting close to her friend as she continued. "We were having a discussion one day in a lesson about immigration and Shay, and I started talking and put two and two together."

"Why did you decide not to tell me?"

Petra looked away into the distance. "It wasn't about you at all. We weren't ready to tell my mum. I thought she'd be upset. When we finally told her, she was so happy and just kept hugging Shay." Petra turned towards Erin and smiled. "I was going to tell you, and then you wouldn't speak to me."

"I'm really sorry. I was so caught up with finding my sister that everything else was just a blur." Erin turned her face to the warmth of the sun, and after a moment or two added, "It's alright Pet."

The sudden push from Petra made Erin almost fall off the bench. "You know I hate that!"

"He calls you Pet."

"Yes, and it's really irritating; just like him. I never understood why you fancied him. He can be a real pain sometimes!"

Erin grinned at this. A memory flashed into her mind. A text from Petra. Her smile vanished, and a shadow fell across her. The sun had disappeared behind a fluffy white cloud, but the shiver down her spine was nothing to do with the coolness of the air. "Why was Shay warning me?"

It was Petra's turn to grin now. "He was saying he knows you like him, and he was trying to warn you that he wasn't interested... because he's gay!"

"How could I have been so stupid not to have seen that?" Erin sighed. "Anyway, after all I've been through, boys are way down on my list of priorities."

"Mine too!" agreed Petra. "I have to admit though, some of those guys from Zephyr are quite cute."

Erin playfully slapped her arm and then began to laugh: a wonderful cathartic feeling that filled her with hope and happiness.

The elegant dark wood table in the dining room was extended to its full length – big enough to seat at least twelve people. Only three were seated there when Erin entered the room. Patrick, Mal and Miranda were engrossed studying various documents, a sea of folders spread out across the polished surface. Erin smiled to see that Patrick had crafted a tiny boat out of a scrap torn from his notebook and it was now floating on an ocean of paper.

He looked up as Erin sat down at the table. "You okay?" he whispered.

She nodded in reply.

Patrick continued in a soft, quiet voice like a librarian and gestured towards a small neat stack of folders. "Those are the folders of you guys and some of the Teardrops." He then pointed to a messy heap of paper and files. "That needs sorting. We haven't found everyone's details yet."

Erin nodded again and began to sift through the mound, trying to make sense of it all. The hours passed. The only sounds in the room were of paper rustling, the scratching of pens and the occasional sigh and gasp as they scanned the information. Bianca brought in coffee and sandwiches which were devoured as they continued to sort.

Finally, Patrick replaced the lid of his pen with a click and stretched his arms above his head. "Shall we review what we've got?"

The air seemed to shift as everyone sat back and eased their stiff shoulders, loosening the tension lying within their muscles. Erin knew this was going to be hard going as she had experienced a little of Zephyr, but what she now saw set down in black and white terrified her. She steeled herself to listen to more horrifying descriptions of how the students of Zephyr had been brought up and educated.

Mal began with what he had discovered. "We have all the paperwork for the Teardrops except for Z59 Augcon, Z28 Maycon and Z46 Novcon, so we don't have their real names or their contact details. However, looking through the documents there seems to be a pattern of specialist subjects and upbringing for each contingent."

Miranda took up the dialogue, "Yes, as you can see, for example, Marcon's specialist subject is science, Febcon's is computing and Augcon's is philosophy." She held up a rough chart she and Mal had produced.

"Interesting," mused Patrick. "You said their upbringing is different too. What do you mean?"

"So far, we haven't found the details of this, but each person has a special mark stamped on their front cover." Mal held it up to show the others. "We weren't sure what this meant to begin with. As you can see, there is either a heart or a broken heart."

"I remember some of my childhood, and it wasn't a lot of fun," Miranda said. "I remember being left in my cot, crying, wanting to be held, but no one came to me. The room was full of crying children. There was no love given to us. There was no time for play or cuddles. The Orderlies came and went with blank, cold faces. They fed and changed us, but we were scolded if we cried and slapped if we tried to touch them. We learned that we didn't need love, that nobody cared about us and that touching was forbidden."

While Miranda opened her heart to them, Erin found her eyes filling with tears as she reflected on her own childhood. Her mum and dad were always there for her, with comfort and warmth in bucketloads. Yes, they clothed and fed her too – these were the only similarities – but the time they gave her, the love they showered upon her, the support and guidance they bestowed on one of their daughters should have been shared between the two girls.

"What about the thing you all say about love?" Mal asked.

Miranda stared at him. "What thing?"

Mal, Patrick and Erin returned her stare. "When you all stand and repeat those words," explained Patrick.

"It's their way of showing they care about us. They tell us it's good for us; to be like a family. It's not though, is it? You're a family, you three and Stella. You might fall out at times, but you show them your love by the little things you do for one another; you support and guide them."

"You're part of our family, Miranda," Patrick said, rising from his chair and going to her. He held out his hand like a star, but Miranda jumped up and wrapped her arms around him.

Erin and Mal followed suit. "Family hug!" Mal shouted.

Pulling apart and looking at their grinning faces, Erin said. "I miss Mum. I wish she were here too; then we'd all be together."

"I know, sweetheart," Patrick muttered. "I'll try her again this afternoon. She's probably at her shop. Summer sale and all that sort of stuff."

"Yeah, I'm sure that's it." Erin returned to her chair while the others did the same. Inwardly, she was worried. Reflecting on what she had learned about Cara's mother being killed in a car accident, her tummy became knotted, twisting and turning.

"Going back to the heart symbol," Mal said pointedly. "We think because Miranda's file has a broken heart, this corresponds to her childhood. Trefoil were experimenting with everyone in Zephyr to see what happened if babies and children were not loved and cared for properly."

"That means some of our Teardrops have had the same experiences as me," Miranda brought her hand to her heart. "And some of them have had a good childhood with love and care."

"It'll be interesting to see how this affects them all, now they're out of that awful institution," Patrick added. "I think we've done enough for today. Why don't we go for a walk to stretch our legs?"

Both Mal and Erin groaned. They knew what their father's walks could be like. Miranda beamed. "That would be lovely."

Erin was worried and not just about having to go for a walk. "Is it safe for us to go out? What if they've found us and are watching the house?"

"I think we'll be okay. Bianca rented the house through someone she knows. Trefoil won't find us here. We're safe, and besides, we're not going far. There's a café halfway up the Wrekin, the hill you

can see from the house. We'll just head for that,"
Patrick said.

"Could we ring Mum from there?" asked Erin.

"Apparently, there's a red telephone box, that's still
in operation, next to the café. We'll try that," Patrick
explained.

"Let's get going!" he added, herding them out of
the room.

TREFOIL HQ

Transcript of Meeting

Oliver Irons: This is the first time we have experienced such rebellion. What are your thoughts on the matter?

Joyce Williams: This has shown weaknesses and strengths.

Oliver Irons: Explain please.

Joyce Williams: As in any experiment there will be weaknesses – aspects you may not have prepared for; results you didn't expect. Through these violations of our system, considerable strengths have been discovered. We are learning by our mistakes, so we will know what to do next time. Our plan was to create a superior race and as a result their intelligence and power is also superior. I believe this has shown we were right in setting up NN2000.

Oliver Irons: So, you are saying we must use this to our own advantage? We require your confirmation of next actions.

Joyce Williams: Of course. Their resistance against our methods shows they can resist people in power. That will help us in the future.

Chapter 12

Miranda surveyed the scene stretched out before her. She was out of breath from the climb, but the view was worth it. An ocean of green fields led away to hills, grey and mysterious, far into the distance.

They discovered the phone box alongside the café. Patrick and Erin squeezed themselves inside the tiny red-framed kiosk while Miranda stood outside watching Mal kick some gravel against a wooden fence.

"Have you heard from Cara?" she asked.

"No."

"Where do you think she is?"

"Dunno. Don't really care."

Miranda didn't know what to say next, so went to look at the menu board outside the café. I'm not very good at this stuff, she thought. I'm not very good at much really, Zephyr saw to that. I don't even know what half these things are on this board. She scanned the cream coloured card, covered with ornate writing. What is a muffin? Eccles cake, pancakes? I know what chocolate cake is, but how do you make a cake out of a pan? She was pondering all of this when a shout from behind her caused her to jump. She twisted round to see Mal pointing across the fields to where a main road cut through the swathes of green.

"Look!" Mal shouted to her.

Three black cars, with their windows blanked out, were making their way along the road. Miranda watched the stately procession; the hair on the back of her neck rising, her heart thumping hard. "Are they here for us?" she asked, not taking her eyes off the predatory vehicles, sharks hunting them down.

"They seem to be going towards the house." Miranda gasped at this, ran to the fence, then leaned over the splintery wood to get a better view. They observed the cars turn right, away from the house and down a side road towards a squat brick building with a corrugated metal roof.

Miranda let out her breath as a loud sigh and then whispered, "What is that place?"

"It looks like a garage where they repair cars." The forecourt in front of the building was littered with old wrecks. Dark green double doors opened as the first car approached them. The three black cars entered the building, and the doors closed behind the third.

Erin ambled over to them, "What are you two looking at?" Patrick trailed after her.

"There were some cars coming down the road, while you were talking to Stella," explained Miranda.

"You mean talking to the answering machine," Erin muttered. "What about them?"

Mal answered quickly. "I don't think it's anything to worry about. They drove into that garage." He pointed to the building.

"So what?" Erin asked, rubbing her arms. Miranda found she was doing the same; a cold wind was winding its way around them.

"There's no one there. The doors opened automatically, and then they vanished. No people have come out." Miranda found her voice cracking with fear. "I think they've come from Zephyr to find us and they've hidden the cars in that garage."

Erin and Mal exchanged a look.

"If we had the Trefoil info, we would've been able to discover more about their organisation," Patrick said.

"That would've been really helpful," agreed Mal. "Actually, I don't think those cars have anything to do with Trefoil. It's just a garage storing cars. What's weird about that?"

"You're right, son. Don't let's jump to conclusions. We have enough to think about as it is."

They started off down the path; Mal and Patrick leading the way, with Miranda and Erin wandering behind.

Erin whispered, "I've got the folder."

Miranda froze. "What do you mean?" she hissed back. She stared at her twin. Erin was standing, eyes cast down, hands in her jeans' pockets.

"Like I said. I have the Trefoil folder. I've hidden it."

"Why haven't you given it to Patrick? What's the matter with you?"

"Shhh! Keep your voice down. They'll hear you."

"You have to tell them. If you don't, I will."

Erin caught Miranda's arm. "Please, don't. I don't know who to trust anymore." She let go abruptly and began to rub her palms up and down her face and then clasp and unclasp her hands. Miranda couldn't believe what she was saying.

"Stop it!" Miranda said, angry with her sister. She grabbed both her hands and stared deep into Erin's steel-grey eyes. "We have to trust Patrick and Mal. They're family. If I can trust them after what my life has been like, then so should you. We must work together."

Erin's whole body seemed to shrink before her eyes. Miranda held her hands tightly. "Trust me, Erin. You're my sister. You and I are one."

"You're right. We must be true to each other and our family. As soon as we get back to the house, I'll get the file."

"Thank you," Miranda murmured.

 Arriving back at the house, they all went their separate ways; Erin making for her small pile of belongings in the conservatory. One positive thing she had learned from Zephyr was she could do without material possessions; people were more important. Thankfully, there was no one around. She knelt, lifting the sleeping bag and pushing her hand down inside the depths of soft fabric, Erin searched blindly for the folder. She couldn't feel the cold metal at all. Unzipping the bag, she saw straightaway there was nothing there. The Trefoil file had gone.

Sitting back on her heels, Erin blew out a breath of air. Where is it? I'm sure I put it in here. It was here this morning. No, wait a minute... I hid it somewhere else... but where? Her mind was all over the place. So much stuff going around her head – Petra – Stella – Miranda – Shay. Think, Erin, she said to herself.

What is it, Mum always says if I can't find anything? Retrace your steps. Right, think! What did I do after I piled up this stuff here? I had breakfast... no before that... what did I do when I first woke up? I had a shower. Okay, let's go back there. Erin walked along the short hallway leading back towards the main house. A wet room was situated near a utility room where a washing machine was busy and a tumble drier hummed. They were both full of grey clothing from the Zephyr students.

I had my shower and then... I remember now... I had taken the folder with me as I couldn't leave it in my sleeping bag and then I... I couldn't take it in while I had a shower as everything gets soaked and then I...oh, this is hopeless. The clothes sloshed back and forth behind the circular window. The clothes... they'd been in a laundry basket... I saw them when I...

Erin ran to the wooden lattice-work chest. She had stuffed the folder down between the canvas bag, full of clothes, and the inside wall of the box. The bag was still inside, hanging loosely on its hooks. Please let it still be here she prayed. Unhooking the bag, Erin slid her arm down inside and groped around with her fingers.

"Looking for something?" Bianca asked, entering the room.

Erin snatched her hand back as though she had been bitten and stood up. "Oh, hi Bianca."

"What's the matter? You look like you've been caught raiding the cake tin." The woman laughed at her own joke and strolled across the room to the drier. After opening the door, she began to pull the dry grey shirts out and into a green basket sitting ready on the floor. The washing machine was now spinning; the clothes twirling round and round.

Erin giggled, but inwardly was squirming. What do I say? "Erm," she began and then stopped.

"You and Petra are so alike." Bianca was now folding the shirts and stacking them on a shelf. "I always know when she's hiding something. Apart from Shay, that is." She chuckled. "That was a huge surprise; a lovely one, though." She turned to Erin. "Did you speak to Stella?"

Erin relaxed; thankful Bianca was like her mum in that she would often forget what they had been talking about. She made her face brighten a little. "No, still no answer. She's probably at the shop." Trying to continue changing the subject, she added, "How's Troy? Where's he staying?"

This was Bianca's favourite subject – her youngest child, Troy. "He's with my parents. I didn't want him affected by all of this." Her gesture looked to Erin like a royal wave, and she began to wonder how Petra's mum really felt about this whole situation. She, like Stella, seemed to want her daughter to stay incarcerated in Zephyr. "He's growing up, Erin. You haven't seen him for a while, have you?" Erin shook her head, wishing now she hadn't chosen this topic.

Bianca continued. "He's the captain of the football and rugby team. Doing very well in school. He took his SATs in May and was brilliant."

When Bianca finally paused for a breath, Erin said quickly, "Can I do anything to help? There's a lot of us here to look after."

"You can say that again!" Bianca smiled, then her face darkened. "I hadn't realised some of them were going to find it hard to adjust. Cassandra and Petra seem to be coping with it all rather well. Tomorrow, can we tell them their names, please? I hate calling them by those awful numbers. I must get on. Would you be a dear and put the washing into the drier, please. The cycle has finished." A beeping sound emitting from the machine agreed with her.

"Yeah, sure." Erin watched Bianca head back to the kitchen.

Running back to the laundry box, Erin leaned in feeling for the file. Her fingernails scraped across a sharp edge. Grasping the metal folder, she tugged it free from its hiding place. Erin stuffed it inside her jumper, before kicking the green basket towards the washing machine and emptying it of its load.

Erin made her way through the kitchen and along to the dining room. Patrick was sitting at the table, studying various papers and making notes in neat handwriting.

"Dad, I need to show you something..." she stopped mid-flow. Frankie and Neal were setting up a computer on a side table. They turned in unison at her voice. "It doesn't matter. I'll come back later." Erin went to close the door, but Patrick rose from his chair.

"You okay?" he asked, removing his glasses and wiping them on his T-shirt. Without turning her head, Erin swivelled her eyes to Frankie and Neal and back again. Patrick nodded. "You're right, sweetheart, it's time to take a break. Let me know when you're ready, guys. Erin and I will be in the garden."

As soon as they were away from the house, Erin pulled the folder out, thankful to remove the hard object and shoved it at Patrick. "I need to give you this. I'm sorry, I should've given it to you straight away."

The sun was setting, the sky flooding with orange and pink, purple and red. The metal reflected the vibrant colours, the Trefoil symbol in the centre, glittering. Patrick didn't speak. Taking the folder, he turned away from her and trudged towards a circular patio within the lawn. Sitting down on one of the wooden chairs, he lay the folder on the round garden table and stared at the image.

Erin hurried over and flung herself down next to him. "Sorry, Dad."

In answer, Patrick reached over and stroked her cheek. "Thank you for finally trusting me, my lovely girl." Erin was alarmed to see tears springing to her father's eyes, and she leaned towards him, hugging him tightly.

"Shall we take a look?" Patrick pulled away from her and patted the cover. Erin was scared to find out what was inside. She swallowed before answering with a slow nod.

The metal file had a simple catch on the side, and it sprang open to Patrick's touch. It was more like a shallow box with various compartments: inside each one was a foam insert moulded to the shape of the item encased there. There were three memory sticks, all covered with a surface of creamy mother of pearl and the Trefoil symbol in gold. In a larger compartment lay a tablet, face down, the cover matching those of the memory sticks.

"Wow," she breathed.

"What beautiful items!" Patrick carefully peeled one of the memory sticks from its skin and began to study it. "This tiny thing could hold all sorts of secrets, Erin."

"Just like Pandora's box," murmured Erin.

"What did you say? Pandora?"

"You know, she's always saying about being careful when opening a box."

Patrick chuckled as he placed the item back in its little bed. "You're right; we must tread carefully."

"Patrick!" A shout from the house cut through the evening air. It was Neal, standing in the courtyard, surrounded by three parts of the building. "Come and see what we've got."

"We'll be right with you!" Patrick replied. Rising from his chair, he stretched out his hand to Erin to help her up. "You know we have to show them this."

Erin glanced at him and nodded. "It's the only way." She grabbed the metal folder and closed it with a click.

Back in the dining room, Erin tried to stifle a yawn, struggling to keep her eyelids open. Neal's mellow voice seemed far away, droning on and on. I must concentrate; this is important. Rubbing her face hard, Erin heaved herself out of her chair and started to pace around the room. The others were still peering at the computer screen, their stone-like faces immobile, with no expression, just pure concentration. All three men, Patrick, Neal and Frankie, were experts in IT and computing. They could finally use their knowledge to help bring down Zephyr and Trefoil.

Neal was explaining the messages transmitted between him and Z11, who he had believed was part of the Teardrops. Erin thought it was just emails, but he went into great detail about how it was a more complex procedure, using all sorts of computer jargon – that was when she switched off.

On the screen were lines of text. The latest message from Z11 was appearing before them.

Z11: Zephyr in LOCKDOWN. Fifteen students have escaped. Miss Dorling removed. Tell me what you know.

On the screen a bright yellow cursor flashed, waiting for an answer.

Neal began tapping in letters, pretending not to know much about an escape.

N: I thought escape had been postponed. How did they get out?

The cursor flashed.

Z11: Gas attack. No one died.

Erin, now standing behind them, breathed out. "Thank goodness."

Neal was tapping on the keyboard once again.

N: What is LOCKDOWN?

Z11: No one can enter or leave Zepyhr. All staff are staying in the school. Trefoil believe people on the inside helped them escape. Staff are being questioned.

N: Do you know who they are? Are you planning another escape?

Z11: We have our suspicions – no real evidence yet. Not planning an escape.

Erin thought of Edward and Professor Hessonite. The latter was back in Zephyr. Would she be in danger now?

N: What is your next step?

Z11: I need to know where the escapees are. Tell me what you know and who you are working for? Are you with Trefoil?

Neal looked across at Patrick, who nodded.

N: I don't know anything. I thought you were part of the escape group.

Z11: No, I am not. Trefoil have already dispatched people to find the escapees. I will be in touch.

The cursor blinked, and the screen went blank. There was silence for a moment before Frankie spoke. "Do you think they'll fall for that?"

"We have to hope so. It might just give us some time." Neal sat back in his chair and clasped his hands behind his head. "I don't know about you guys, but I'm pure done in. My bed's calling me."

"I agree," Patrick added, standing up and moving the chair back to its place at the table. "We have a lot to do tomorrow, including... studying this." He held up the metal folder with a flourish.

"Where d'you find that?" Neal asked, his eyes narrowing as he frowned.

Erin decided to come clean. "I had it. I... erm..."

Patrick interrupted her. "What Erin is trying to say, is that she kept it safe. The four of us will meet here after breakfast and examine the contents."

Neal looked sideways at Frankie, who shrugged in agreement. "Yeah, sure. We can do that." He turned to Erin and hissed, "You'd better keep it safe tonight then, hadn't you. We don't want to lose it, do we?"

Patrick took charge. "It's sleeping with me tonight," he said marching out, throwing a good night back to the others. Neal strode after him, leaving Erin and Frankie to wend their way around the table to the door. Erin went to leave, but Frankie slammed the door shut and stood, arms crossed barring her way.

"What's going on, Erin? Don't you trust me?"

Erin stood her ground. "I don't know what you're talking about. I'm tired. Can you open the door, please?"

"Not until we have this out, Erin." Frankie's voice was sharp, matching his eyes, but then they softened. "You trusted me in Zephyr when you didn't know who I was. What's changed?"

Erin turned away, not wanting to look into his eyes again. "Nothing's changed. I still feel the same as I did in Zephyr."

"What is it then?"

Erin held her breath and closed her eyes, hoping it would make him vanish. She felt electricity going through her arm, and on opening her eyes, she saw he was still there, and now his hand was resting lightly on her shoulder.

"It's Miranda," she whispered.

"What's Miranda got to do with how you feel about me?"

"I didn't know she loved you." Erin stepped back and stumbled to a chair where she fell onto its soft cushioned seat.

"How do *you* feel about me?" Frankie asked, still hovering by the door.

"I don't want to tell you, because the last time I told someone I liked them it backfired." Erin studied her fingernails, bitten and broken, just like she felt.

"I like you both very much. Miranda has a soft vulnerability about her, but an intelligence and intuition that makes her strong. I'm very fond of her because we've both experienced the Zephyr experiments. You, on the other hand, have a resilience, a strength I admire. You have a fire in your belly that can help make a difference to all those young people. I like that... I need that, but not in the way you hoped. I'm sorry, Erin. I need you and Miranda beside me to finish this, to finish what Trefoil started."

"To trust you completely, I have to know who you are. Who *did* visit you at the end of each five-year phase?"

"It wasn't the professor. Two grey-haired people came. They were kind and gentle towards me. The lady had twinkly eyes, and the man's skin was very wrinkly, like old leather."

"Perhaps they were your grandparents." Erin stood and walked around the table to the pile of folders. "Do you want to know?" she asked, holding up a folder with Z42 and a broken heart symbol on the front.

Frankie's eyes suddenly filled with tears. "I don't know," he stuttered. Erin's heart softened. He does have feelings, she thought.

Laying the folder down on the table, she opened the flap and pulled out various sheets of paper. Reading out loud from the top sheet, Erin said, "Designated visitors at five-year phases are as follows: NJ and EE Whitstone. Unrelated to child. Assigned to Z42 by father as mother is deceased. Oh, Frankie, I am sorry."

"Keep going, please. Is my name Frankie? The two people used to call me that, but I don't know who's telling the truth. I have to know. Please tell me, Erin."

Erin took a deep breath and continued to read from the sheet. "Mother – Jessica; Father – Douglas; Sibling – Cara; Twin – George; True name – Franklyn; Surname – Mallory."

"Well, that's that then. I know who I am." Frankie looked to Erin as though all the life had been punched out of him.

"So, they've been telling the truth all along," sighed Erin returning the papers into the folder. What if they're also in danger and were taken against their will? She mused.

Pulling out a chair, Frankie plonked himself down and said, "Forget my family; I never really knew them; they never cared about me." He paused and then added, "I do recognise certain traits in them and in myself; our nature, I suppose. To really trust me, I want to tell you what I know and what I believe in."

Erin sat down and waited for him to continue.

"I was about ten years old when I realised; I had a gift," he said. "We were studying in the Learning Lab, and I had finished the task, so I began to experiment to see what I could do with the computer. From that day, I honed my skills and knowledge. I accessed information on Zephyr and what was going on in there. I used that information to approach a range of students each with a different subject knowledge – their gift. When we entered Zephyr, we were chosen because of our families: their backgrounds, their expertise. Trefoil studied the education of our parents and grandparents because they were testing whether it's nature or nurture that is the strongest; NN2000 is the title of their project."

Erin nodded; this matched with what Miss Dorling had told her. "Yes, I know. What else have you learned?"

"One thing I have learned is…" he stopped and stood up. "… that if our bodies don't rest properly, we are rubbish the next day." He grinned and reached out his hand towards Erin in a gentlemanly manner. "Erin, please trust me. I am a true Teardrop having shed more tears than anyone. I am here to help you and your family, my family and me, but most of all those who are still in Zephyr and their families. They are all being duped into believing they are doing the right thing. Trefoil are evil; the people who run the organisation must be stopped. I believe they're part of a much bigger plan, but I still don't know what that is."

Erin rose from her seat and in answer reached out, her hand formed into the teardrop shape.

Frankie raised his hand to hers, and together they formed a butterfly.

"Let's make those butterflies go free... tomorrow!" Erin said and made her way to the door. Once there, she turned. "I trust you, Frankie, but if you ever double-cross my family or me, I will hunt you down."

Frankie grinned. "I know you would! I wouldn't expect any other response from you."

They left the room together, laughing, but Erin felt a shiver as she switched off the lights and closed the door behind her. I'm still on my guard. I'm still ready for betrayal by someone, whoever it is.

MESSAGE

To: Trefoil

From: Z11

Have made contact with N. He/she does not seem to know much about the escape from Zephyr. We are trying to pinpoint the location of N but there is something preventing this within the system we are currently using.

I will contact N again and this time try to ascertain more about who he/she is working with. I suspect Z42 is the leader of the Teardrops. I will ask N if they have been in contact.

I await further action from you.

Chapter 13

Miranda finished folding her piece of paper just before Patrick did the same. They swapped the two boats and studied the folds.

"Hmmm, not bad, I suppose," Miranda pronounced. "A bit slow, though."

Patrick smiled at this riposte. "You're quick, I grant you, but your folds aren't very sharp."

Miranda gazed at him. "Excuse me," she spluttered. "You were my only teacher in this, so you are at fault here." She kept her face deadpan, no emotion. Patrick's smile vanished, and he looked horror-stricken at having upset her. Miranda couldn't keep a straight face for much longer, and the laughter she was holding inside suddenly burst out in a glorious chuckle.

Patrick's echoing guffaw made everyone in the kitchen look across at them, which made them giggle even more.

"When you two have finished with your origami, can we get on please?" Bianca's sensible voice wafted over to the two of them. They waited for her to look away and then both raised a salute, which set the two of them howling again.

Miranda bathed in the warmth of the joy emanating between herself and this dear man. Memories of sitting opposite him in the dining room in the hotel came to her in waves. His gentle eyes, the way he rubbed his bearded chin when he was thinking, his intelligence and humour and his love for life. In the same instance, the sad eyes of Stella appeared, haunting her and bringing sorrow and regret. Where is she? Why is she not replying to their calls? Miranda didn't feel so close to Stella as she did to Patrick, and she wanted that same closeness.

Nudging Patrick, she asked, "Do you think someone should go and visit Stella and check she's okay?"

"I'm sure she's fine."

"Please, could someone go and check on her."

Patrick looked across at his youngest daughter. "Mal could go, I suppose. I'll ask him."

"Thank you, Pat… Dad." Miranda gave a hopeful smile and Patrick, his eyes lighting up enveloped her in a big hug.

"Of course, my lovely girl. Anything for you."

They made their way to the living room, their two paper boats lying forgotten on the table, one upright soaking up a pool of spilt tea, the other marooned on a plate full of crumbs, like sharp rocks in the sea, ready to puncture the hull of a boat.

Later, Miranda sat in the living room listening to Patrick and Neal telling everyone the plans for the day.

Through the plate-glass windows, she watched heavy rain pounding the trees and shrubs, their leaves and flowers bowing down, disconsolate and forlorn. The summer sunshine had been washed away. She thought of Mal driving in this awful weather and hoped he would be alright. He had been surprised to be asked to drive down to Buckinghamshire to see Stella, but after Patrick had explained everything to him, he understood. Bianca calmly handed him the keys to her car when he protested: he had no wheels. They had all hugged him briefly before waving him off. Now, Patrick was telling all the Teardrops about the individual meetings they were going to hold today. They wanted to speak to each one, in turn, informing them of their real name and finding out how they were coping with the change of environment.

The meeting was over, and the Teardrops left the room. "Miranda, will you come with me, please? Erin, can you sit with Neal?" Patrick spoke with conviction. "I drew this up last night. We'll be in the small sitting room at the front of the house and will see these people." He indicated some names and numbers on a list he held in his hand. "Erin and Neal, you'll be in the study. Here's your list." He handed over another piece of paper to Erin.

"Unfortunately, we are missing the documents for three of the students, Z59, Z28 and Z46. Miranda and I will talk to the three of them together."

"What about me?" Frankie asked. "What shall I do?"

"Frankie, I'd like you to communicate with Z11. See if you can find out a bit more about what's

PAPER BOATS & BUTTERFLIES

happening with the lockdown. Also, contact Pandora and check on Edward and Professor Hessonite."

The young man nodded and then scratched his thatch of red hair; it had been a few days since his last head-shave, and the spikes of flame added a warmth to his pale face. Miranda threw a smile at him as they went their separate ways.

Once they were seated, Patrick passed her the list, and she scanned it quickly. "I'll go and find Z77 Marcon," she said, leaping up in her hurry to get going.

"Wait a minute, Miranda." She paused with her hand frozen above the door handle.

"Yes?"

"Are you okay with all of this? It might be upsetting for you as well as them."

Miranda lowered her hand and turned slowly to face him. "I want them to be with their family, just like me. Education is important, but not when it damages the soul of a person. Being loved and nurtured by your family is more important." Pausing, before shrugging her shoulders, she added. "Well, that's what I think, anyway."

Patrick grinned. "Okay, good. But talk to me if you need help."

Miranda shrugged again and pulled open the door before hurrying off towards the games room, hoping to find Z77 Marcon there. Entering the large room at the back of the house, where a pool table, darts board and TV were all in use, she was pleased to find Erin already there in some discussion with two of the boys. Coming closer, the conversation was becoming quite animated, and Erin's voice was growing louder. "That's not how you play pool!" she was saying to them. "Let me show you." Erin walked across to a wooden frame on the wall with long wooden rods attached to it.

Miranda watched with amusement as Erin continued. "You hit the balls in with one of these." She held up a stick. "This is called a cue. You don't just push them in with your fingers or hands." Miranda smirked as she watched her sister, demonstrate how to hit the balls into the pockets. Erin pocketed three balls one after the other. "Voila!" she finished triumphantly. The boys excitedly grabbed a cue each and tried to do the same, but with little success.

Erin left them to it and joined Miranda. "They have absolutely no idea," she said.

"Give them time. They'll work it out."

"Who are you looking for?" Erin asked. "I need Z64 Sepcon, and I don't know her at all."

"She's over there." Miranda pointed across to a group of girls who were all reading from a pile of women's magazines. "Z64, can you please go to the study with Erin?" The girl who stood was beautiful, her face and neck seemed to have been created by a master sculptor from obsidian; angular cheekbones accentuating her almond-shaped eyes. She did not smile; she just acknowledged them both with a shift of her head and strode out of the room; Erin hurrying after her.

Miranda glanced across at a young man sitting on a bench by himself, deep in thought until she called him. Looking up to see who had uttered his name, he blushed and turned away.

"Hi, Z77. How are you?" she said.

"I'm w-w-well, th-th-thank you."

"Would you please come with me, as we have some information about your family." Miranda gestured towards the open door, and the young man inclined his head in assent.

The two of them left the room in silence and made their way to the sitting room where Patrick was waiting. "Hello there," Patrick said, pointing to an empty chair. The boy sat on the edge of the seat; his legs close together with his elbows resting on his thighs.

"Hi Patrick. How are you?" he said, smiling.

Miranda was astonished. No stutter or shyness, no redness came to his face. She wondered why he was so different towards Patrick.

"I'm good, thanks. Okay, we have managed to find out your real name and where your family live."

"Yes, that's good," Z77 responded.

Patrick looked down at a pile of papers before saying, "Your name is Lucas...Lucas Stone and your family live in a place called Bath."

In the silence that followed, Miranda and Patrick waited patiently before Z77 spoke. "That's nice. I like that. Will you please call me Lucas from now on?"

"Yes, of course," said Miranda brightly. The boy glanced across at her and his face flushed.

"Th-th-thank you." His stutter was back.

"Here's your file. You can study it while Miranda collects the next person." Patrick handed the thin folder over to Lucas.

Leaving the room, Miranda caught snatches of a question Lucas was putting to Patrick. "Why... broken heart... cover?" In her mind's eye, she saw a little boy sitting in a cot, facing the wall, not crying, never speaking, just silent.

The next person to collect was Z91 Febcon. Her real name was Bella Norton, and Miranda looked forward to her learning her name and about her family. Z91 was often quick to support her own views when they had debates in Zephyr, and she seemed to be someone who could now become a friend. Miranda soon found her in the living room, watching a film with several others. Z91's eyes lit up on seeing Miranda, and she quickly clambered up from the cushions on the floor. She talked incessantly as they walked over to the sitting room, asking questions, talking about the film and enquiring when it was time for lunch.

The morning flew by. The Teardrops found out their names and appeared to really enjoy sharing this with the others. Bianca had made badges, but no one chose to wear them. Instead, they savoured the names they had heard briefly at each five-year phase and were now being confirmed as their true identity. None of them had been aware this day was the day of their birth and were astonished to hear how birthdays were celebrated in the real world.

Each of the Teardrops was given an opportunity to say how they were coping with these new experiences. Some were enjoying their new-found freedom and already were looking forward to meeting their families, but others were frightened. They were experiencing awful nightmares and were overwhelmed by all the new things they had never seen before. A couple of the students even wanted to go back to Zephyr. Miranda understood this. To come out of somewhere you know, even though it can be painful at times, is a huge step. It was the unknowing that was frightening.

The three students, whose papers hadn't been found, were able to tell Patrick what they thought their first name was, having been referred to by a certain name, at their five-year phases. Z59 was known as Aaron, Z28 Emiko and Z46 was Deana.

Patrick and Miranda had been able to ascertain from each of the Teardrops they always had two people who visited them, but on checking their file, some of them had sadly lost their actual parents or their twin. It was recorded that aunts, uncles, grandparents or nominated persons came to visit, and it was always one man and one woman.

After a morning of seeing various people, Miranda went along to the kitchen and stared out at the heavy granite sky. She began to wonder if this had been the best way of fighting against Zephyr and Trefoil. They couldn't stay in this beautiful house forever. For her, this had been a special time with her family, but to continue with whatever Frankie and the Teardrops had started, they had to all take the next step. Patrick and Neal were already contacting families about their children; with the lack of mobile phones and only contacting safe people via a computer they had decided to do it the old way – by writing to them.

Lunch was being served behind her; sandwiches piled up on plates, a huge bowl of fruit, more plates with fruit cake and scones and several glass jugs of orange and apple juice. People came and took what they wanted and found somewhere to sit and eat. Miranda wasn't hungry and studied the raindrops slipping and sliding down the glass.

A flash of bright orange caught her eye and glancing through the window again, Patrick could be seen dashing down the winding drive towards the road. His orange water-proof coat was zipped up against the weather, and he held a package under his arm. He was on his way to the phone box to try and get hold of Stella and to post all the letters. Miranda thought he was mad as she watched him splashing through the puddles and giggled to herself. He's going to be soaked! That was one good thing about Zephyr, it never rained!

"He's crazy, isn't he?" said Erin sidling up to her. "Going out in this weather!"

They stood side by side, staring out at the spears of rain, their faces lighting up with a sudden flash of lightning. A distant grumble of thunder followed, and the girls reached out to grasp each other's hand.

Erin loved a good thunderstorm. She had tried so many times to film lightning, but to no avail. Once we're back home again, I'm going to save up to buy a decent camera, she decided. She couldn't wait for all this to be over. The morning had been exhausting with some students becoming distressed on sight of their files. She wondered if they should have brought them out of Zephyr, a place where they felt safe, a place she would never comprehend as being anything but dangerous. They had opened a 'can of worms' as her grandma would say, and now they had to face the consequences.

A tap on her shoulder made her swing round, letting go of her sister's hand. It was Frankie. "Oh, it's you," she said.

"I need to show you and Patrick something. Do you know where he is?"

"He's gone for a run."

"In this? He's mad!" exclaimed Frankie.

"We know!" added Miranda. "What is it?"

Frankie began to pull at their arms. "Come with me. You must see this." Erin waved his hands away but consented to follow him. On entering the dining room, Erin saw the Trefoil box had been tampered with.

"What have you done?" Erin said, her voice beginning to rise.

"It's okay. Patrick and Neal asked me to see if I could get it working. Look at the screen." Frankie held up the tablet; the three memory sticks were all protruding from the top edge.

"Wow! That's quite something! I've never seen anything like that before," Erin exclaimed going to touch one of the sticks before Frankie pulled her hand away. "Do you have to have all three in there for it to work, Frankie?"

"Don't touch them! I had to put them in the correct order to make it work. It took a while I can tell you; there are various configurations. I've now numbered them." Tiny stickers clearly marked the sequence.

"What have you looked at so far?" Erin asked, gazing at the screen. There was a silver trefoil outline on a black background, with a graphic of a white pyramid spinning in its centre surrounded by several triangles of different colours forming a geometric pattern.

"I've clicked on some of them. The different triangles indicate the different aspects of Trefoil; some show pictures and maps of places - the spinning shape in the centre just shows an empty room - nothing very exciting. This one has information about Zephyr and their educational aims." He quickly touched the red one, and more triangles shot from it like a firework exploding in the night sky and settled across the screen, each one emblazoned with a title.

"There are various reports from Esme Dorling to three people – John Johnson, Joyce Williams and Oliver Irons. I think the three of them work for Trefoil." Frankie touched a white triangle, and the reports appeared on the screen.

"It looks like Miss Dorling got into trouble over your escape," said Miranda.

"Look, they knew about Mal being in hospital!" exclaimed Erin.

"They've been following our every move, but thankfully they don't seem to have ascertained where we are now," Frankie explained. He returned the screen back to the original one and placed his finger ready to touch the blue triangle. "This one gives us more detailed information about where they're based and how they work."

"I think we should wait for Patrick and Neal before we look at the rest of them, don't you, Miranda?" Erin said.

Miranda nodded and started to say something when the door was flung open, and Patrick squelched in. All three of them whipped around, guilt on their faces. "She's gone!" he shouted, water dripping from his beard, tears mixing with raindrops. Erin stared at the vision that was her father. Steam was rising from his shoulders as though his spirit was materialising and leaving his body. A shiver ran down her spine. For a moment, time was suspended – the drip-drip-drip of water resounded on the wooden floor. Then, as though someone had pressed the fast-forward button on a remote, they all moved and spoke at the same time.

"What?" "When?" "How do you know?" The voices merged into one; they all rushed forward to pull Patrick in, to sit him down, to help him remove his sodden anorak.

"Mal... I spoke with Mal... the house... the house has been turned over..." Patrick sprawled in a chair; all the fight gone from him.

At the same moment, a wavering, ghostly voice pervaded the room. "My name is Stella Winslow."

Shocked at hearing her mother's voice, Erin twisted round to see where it was coming from. On the screen of the Trefoil tablet, she could see a shot of a room. Coming closer to study it, she could make out a table with a sharp tapered point aimed towards... Stella.

"Oh my God!" she screamed. "Dad, look!"

Everyone crowded around the screen and watched in horror as the scene unfolded before them.

"How did you get this?" Patrick asked.

"I had my finger ready to click on the screen," explained Frankie. "When you came in like that the shock must have made me jog my hand. This was an empty room when I looked at it earlier. I'm sorry. I don't know what to say."

"Shhh!" whispered Miranda. "Look this is in real-time, this isn't a recording."

Silently they all pulled a chair up to the screen, sat down and waited.

Erin could see her mum was scared, her eyes, red from crying, had a haunted look. She wasn't dressed in her usual designer clothing; she wore stained jeans and a torn shirt, her feet were bare and black with dirt. Her hair, usually in an immaculate bob, was tangled and unkempt. Where is she? Mum, I'm so sorry. I'm to blame for all this.

"You, Stella Winslow, have been brought here to explain yourself." A voice boomed out, an educated voice, a voice that spoke of public schools and of Oxbridge. Erin realised there were two people sitting either side of the pointed table, a man to the right and a woman to the left, neither of whom had spoken. A third person - who couldn't be seen by the camera - could be heard clearly asking, "What can you tell us?" It was the same well-spoken voice.

"I don't know how I can help you," Stella stuttered, shoulders bowed as though she carried the weight of the whole world. "I don't know where they are."

Erin reached out to Patrick's arm for support. "They're asking her about us, aren't they?"

"Yes," he whispered back, stretching his other hand out to cover Erin's.

"How dare you let this happen! What have you done with our children? Their parents are anxious for them to be returned as soon as possible." This was from the woman, her voice growing shrill with her accusations. Her profile showed an aquiline nose and porcelain skin with blonde hair piled above a high forehead. She was dressed in pure white. While waiting for the answer, Erin cast her eyes across to the man on the right of the screen. He also wore pure white clothing, but his face was rugged, the skin pockmarked above a rough beard and thick, curly brown hair skimmed his shoulders.

"I don't know. I didn't know this was going to happen. Esme... Miss Dorling told me Erin was very talented and has a high IQ. I thought she'd be safe. We took in her artwork to show the principal. We were told she could finish her education there and leave at 18 with a chance to do great things. We thought this was the best thing to do at the time." Stella began to shake; she held her head in her hands and shouted, "I never wanted her to escape!"

Erin gasped at this cold confession by her mother. Patrick patted her hand and said, "She's only saying this to protect you. She doesn't mean it."

The bearded man in white leaned forward. "You and your ignorant family have caused disruption to our plans. Every moment you waste – not telling us what we want to know - costs us money. We don't like waste… we don't like wasting money. We have warned you time and time again…"

With a loud cry, Stella collapsed on the floor. The discernible plea, "Don't hurt them, don't hurt my babies, please…" audible through her loud anguished sobs.

"Lock her up!" The first voice came again, authoritative, strong, forceful.

Erin tightened her hold on Patrick's arm. "Dad, they can't do this. This is illegal. It's inhumane. We have to stop them!"

Patrick replied by taking her in his arms and rocking her. "It's alright, my lovely girl," he crooned. "Don't worry. Your mum's made of strong stuff. Where do you think you get your strength and determination from?"

Another set of arms embraced them. Erin was surprised to find Frankie, holding them tight in a bear hug. "I promise we'll get her out," he murmured in a hushed tone.

Untangling herself, Erin watched her mother being dragged away – she disappeared from the view of the camera, which continued to roll - leaving the two visible people sitting at the triangular table.

"For our second item on the agenda," the woman in white declared. "We will be looking into and comparing Zephyr, Terra, Aqua and Ignis."

"Yes, it's time to compare progress," the man in white added.

"After the debacle of Zephyr, we need to ensure our schools are safe and our educational aims are not impeded," the woman continued.

Erin listened in horror, trying to make sense of their words. There are other schools! Zephyr's not the only one. What if they're all as bad in how they treat young people? The realisation of what they were up against wrenched all the air from her lungs, and she felt faint.

As though the disembodied voice had read her thoughts, an answer came. "We must continue the experimentation and metamorphosis in all our schools. We will stay on schedule."

"Thought Reform has commenced in all the schools," added the man in white. "Soon we will have a workforce of which our country can be proud."

The person who remained hidden handed around various papers. Stretching across the table caused the sleeve of his white clothing to ride up, revealing a red and orange mark on his left wrist. "Take some time now to read and inwardly digest the information. We will reconvene in one hour's time. Remember we must ensure that everything is ready for November 2018."

The two people in white stood in unison and left the table, without speaking, each one taking a stack of paper with them.

The four people observing the meeting were silent, absorbing everything they had witnessed.

Patrick was the first to speak. "Right everyone, we have an hour. We need to find out where they're holding Stella."

"Most of what we need is on here," said Frankie. "I can take you through it."

"Thank you, Frankie, but I'd like to investigate this further myself," Patrick said, pointing to the tablet. "Erin, can you stay here with me please." Erin nodded. "Frankie and Miranda, I need you to contact Mal. See if he's found any clues at the house. Ask him to speak to any neighbours who might have seen something."

Miranda smiled and nodded, "Of course, happy to help." Patrick shoved his hand into a pocket of his jacket, still damp from the rain, and pulled out a plastic card and some money. "Here, you'll need these. Just follow the instructions in the phone box, and you'll be okay." He grabbed a piece of paper from the table, scribbled down some numbers and passed this across to her.

Frankie lumbered over to the door, his shoulders drooping, his face set in a frown. Miranda followed him, stuffing everything into her jeans' pocket. On opening the door, leading to the spacious hallway, they encountered Neal carrying a tray of steaming mugs and a plate of cakes.

"Perfect timing," he said, entering the room and placing the tray on the table. "I thought you'd be in here. There's been a wee problem – a couple of the kids went off on one, and we've been trying to calm them down." He stood surveying the scene. "What's happened?"

"We're fine, but Stella isn't," announced Miranda, grabbing some cake. "Come on Frankie, let's go, we don't have much time." Then seeing his face, took control. "Stop moping. We must all do our bit. You've been brilliant getting us this far. We have an important job to do."

Frankie followed her out; his face remained sullen.

Erin grabbed coffee and cake. "You're a lifesaver, Neal. You must have read my mind."

Patrick was already studying the triangles on the screen and took the proffered mug from Erin without looking up.

"Can I help?" Neal asked.

Patrick filled him in on what they had seen, and Neal immediately pulled up a chair. "We have to do this in a logical way," Patrick said. Erin grabbed a pad of paper and a pen and waited.

"We'll open each one in turn and check the contents. Erin, if you jot down key things in each section, then we know where we are."

"Frankie said the blue one had information about Trefoil and where it might be based," Erin added.

"Let's start there then." Pressing on the blue triangle, a myriad of blue triangles just like butterflies flew out and settled on the screen showing off their titles.

TREFOIL HQ

Bulletin

To: Oliver Irons

From: Joyce Williams

Our guests were complaining of the cold and limited space in the triangular holding cells in the top building.

They have now been moved to the larger guest rooms in the basement where they have a bed and other necessities.

We require your confirmation of next actions.

"Take care, Mal," Miranda said.

"You too," Mal said, and then the phone went dead.

Miranda pushed open the door and made her way across to where Frankie was leaning against a fence, looking out across the fields. She pointed out the old garage to him where they had seen the three black cars. There was no one to be seen in the vicinity of the building. The rusting vehicles were sprouting long grass and bright red poppies. Nature taking over, using the empty metal shells as a nursery for seeds dropped there by the breeze.

"What now?" Frankie murmured.

"We'd best get back."

They ran down the track to the main road skirting the hill; Frankie being much faster, reached the bottom before Miranda. Before she could warn him to look for traffic, Frankie stepped out onto the tarmac to head back towards the house. A red flash flew past him, kicking up loose shingle and firing it at his face; Frankie flung himself into the ditch parallel to the road.

Miranda ran to him as he was hauling himself out. "Are you okay?"

Frankie dusted himself down, nodded and limped off down the road.

Miranda looked back, but the vehicle was long gone. A sudden chill swept her body; she had seen that car before.

Having examined most of the files on the tablet, they were beginning to wonder if they would ever find the location of the Trefoil headquarters. Neal had left them to it after Bianca had knocked on the door to ask for some help; a couple of the boys were getting upset, and she needed him to talk to them.

Erin studied her notes. They had learned there was a board of directors who ensured everything was being followed correctly. The curriculum studied at Zephyr was documented, showing each of the Contingents had a subject they were gifted in, physics, biology, languages etc. There were various reports from Esme Dorling to Trefoil and vice versa as well as transcripts of meetings held at Trefoil headquarters. There were maps and plans: a map of Bodmin Moor; a plan of Zephyr when it was a nuclear bunker and an up-to-date plan of what Zephyr looked like now.

Several doodles now surrounded her scribbled notes and turning the paper to examine them from a different angle, Erin suddenly exclaimed, "It's a flame!"

"What's that, love?" Patrick was preoccupied with opening the green triangle and watching tiny green triangles flutter across the screen, like leaves blown by the wind.

"Nothing, really. I saw a mark on that man's arm. The one we couldn't see. I think it's maybe a tattoo in the shape of a flame." She held up her doodles so her dad could see. He gave a cursory glance and then turned back to the screen.

"Aah! This looks more hopeful," he said, pressing the triangle labelled Trefoil Lodge. "Oh! Probably not." He sighed as an image of a historic building came into view. "Just another thing to confuse us," he added, rubbing his beard thoughtfully.

"Wait!" she said, reaching out to stop him from moving to a different file. "Look at the patterns on the walls; they're similar to the card left behind by Trefoil. Those are trefoils surrounding triangles."

"They're windows, I think," added Patrick, enlarging the image.

"The roof has three raised triangles. One of which... has a Trefoil symbol replicated in stone." Erin quickly sketched some of the patterns on her pad of paper.

"You think this is their headquarters. It can't be. This is a historical building; in fact, I think it's not far from Newton," said Patrick. "I wish I could google it. If only I had my phone."

"Me too," Erin agreed. "But we can't so we have to use other methods. I'll go and see if Bianca and Neal have a map."

When Erin returned to the dining room, clutching a dog-eared road atlas of the UK, she found Frankie speaking to Patrick, while Miranda hovered to one side of them.

"No clues. We suggested for Mal to stay put and we'll contact him this evening once we've watched the meeting. Has it started yet?" Pulling up a chair, Frankie made himself comfortable.

"Nothing yet. They've been longer than an hour, though," Patrick answered sitting down next to Frankie. Miranda and Erin stood behind the two men to see the screen more clearly.

"Do you know where she is... where they are?" asked Miranda, leaning on the back of the chair.

Erin described what they had seen, the images and plans. "We didn't look through everything, but we've got some ideas..."

"Shhh! Someone's coming in!" hissed Frankie.

The camera view automatically widened until more of the room could be seen. Four people, all dressed in purple, were entering through a door set at an angle to the rest of the room. Two of the four were women, one of whom was Esme Dorling and they strode purposefully across the screen to two high-backed chairs against the white, highly polished wall. The two men walked towards the two identical chairs on the right of the screen. They all remained upstanding.

Nobody had long to wait before two figures entered, the two people they'd seen before, dressed in sharp white clothing. The wooden table could now be seen fully, a solid piece of oak formed into a pyramid balanced on one point on a wooden, triangular plinth.

The rustle of clothing, accompanied by soft footsteps, and the screech of chair legs could be heard off-camera. Then, adding to the symphony of sound, a deep solo voice rang out. "Welcome to you all. Please sit."

Everyone who could be seen on the screen did as they were told, and all of them remained stiffly upright against the carved oak chairs.

Erin shifted; her back was aching. The road atlas, still in her hand, forgotten.

"It is marvellous to see the Principals of Trefoil's four schools here today." The four in purple bowed their heads as each name was announced. "Esme Dorling of Zephyr, Angela De Vate of Aqua, Ian Adare of Terra and David Core of Ignis."

Erin nudged her father and whispered in his ear, "That woman looks like Aunt Angela, Mum's sister."

Patrick whispered back, "She looks nothing like her. You're imagining things."

The voice continued. "We have come to a point in our project, NN2000, where we need to re-assess our overall plans." It was still the person hidden from the camera who was speaking. "The project has been compromised."

At this, three of the four purple figures uttered a gasp, their eyes glancing from side to side and then latching onto the serene figure of Esme Dorling. Erin lifted her chin in response to seeing the woman, whom she loathed, and hoping she would be the one to receive punishment now.

The well-educated voice came again. "Trefoil have studied the records of all four schools and most of what you are doing is satisfactory. But..." A hand came into view and was slammed down on the table to emphasise his point. "… that is not good enough for what we want these young people to do in the future. We expect excellence at all costs."

The woman dressed in white now spoke. "In order to continue with our plan, we must maintain standards and ensure that all our students are with us on our mission to change the future of this country." She summoned Esme Dorling with a click of her fingers.

The principal of Zephyr rose and walked to the centre of the room, facing the camera. Just where Mum had been standing, thought Erin. She smiled inwardly. This is it! Miss Dorling was going to be punished.

"I am very proud of everything we have achieved at Zephyr," Miss Dorling began. "Our students have proved they are worthy of respect and reward. They have demonstrated great intelligence and imagination." She stood, her head erect and proud, her hands clasped together.

Erin waited to see what Trefoil's response would be to this statement.

The hidden voice boomed out, "Continue."

Miss Dorling raised her eyes directly at the camera. "Before I go on, we must, of course, welcome the family of Stella Winslow to our meeting."

Just as a wave of the sea picks up flotsam and jetsam, all heads turned, all faces glaring at the camera. Erin swallowed; they were looking into her very soul.

"You didn't really think you were safe, did you? Whatever lead you to that idea?"

Erin found herself tightening her grip on the back of the chair. "Dad? What's happening?"

"I will tell you what's happening, girl." Miss Dorling snarled. "You will pay for what you have done to me and my reputation... and my face!" Livid red scars on her face and arms from the glass shards made her look like an evil doll, poorly stitched together.

"If you can hear us, then listen to me," said Patrick. "Don't threaten my family. Return my wife, unscathed and..."

Esme Dorling cut him off. "Look at you. You have become complacent, lazy, sitting around in your lovely house – playing at being the saviours of the Teardrops."

Frankie leaned in towards the screen. "How do you know about us?"

"Ah, Z42, how nice to see you," Miss Dorling sneered. "As soon as you worked out how to use the Trefoil Communication System, we knew exactly where you were. You think you are so clever and of course, you are because we have trained you, nurturing you to your full potential." The syrupy voice oozed into the room.

"What are we going to do, Frankie?" Miranda whispered, hoping the people on the screen couldn't hear her. In answer, he rose and placed his hand on her shoulder.

"We are going to fight!" he shouted.

Patrick echoed Frankie's call to arms. "Yes, we will fight to keep our children free..."

A loud hammering on the front door and shouts from outside broke the air. "OPEN UP! We have you surrounded!"

Patrick stood up so fast, his chair toppled back; Erin moved out of the way before it could fall against her legs. Shouting and screaming now issued from all over the house, and she stepped closer to Patrick for support.

A cacophony of raucous laughter emanated from the screen. "There's no escape. You will never escape from Trefoil!" The hidden voice rang out.

"That's what you think!" Patrick yelled, grabbing the tablet and pulling out each of the memory sticks. Handing one to each of the young people, he tucked the tablet under his arm. "Let's go!" Erin, Miranda and Frankie followed him out to the large square-shaped hallway, the stairs sweeping up to the next floor. Neal and some of the Teardrops were looking down over the bannister, demanding to know what was going on.

"No time to explain. Just get everyone out!" Patrick shouted. "I'll head them off." He ran to the door. "I'll be with you in a minute," he shouted towards whoever was hidden by the huge piece of white oak.

The banging of the door started up again, accompanied by a strident voice. "Open up. NOW!"

"Go!" shouted Patrick, waving his arms at his friend. "Find the others and Bianca." At this, Neal and his companions fled down the stairs and through to the kitchen.

Miranda and Frankie ran through to the back of the house, towards the games room, some of the students following them. There were several doors leading out to the garden. Erin watched them go until her father opened the front door.

"ERIN! This way. Quick!" It was Petra. Erin turned and could see her friend hiding in some bushes. Petra was wildly waving her arms. "Come on!" she shouted.

Erin took one last look at the sea of faces and mouthing a sorry; she ran to Petra.

TREFOIL HQ

Bulletin

- The prisoner, Stella Winslow, has now been transferred to Terra School, The Wrekin, Shropshire.

- Initiate Thought Reform immediately.

Chapter 15

Miranda and Frankie stumbled along a muddy path, winding through trees and shrubs. They had already traversed a field and climbed walls and fences, hiding in the shelter of an old sheep hut to catch their breath. Now, they were in deep woodland. The earlier rain made the emerald greens and burnt ochres sparkle in the evening sunshine. A thick earthy scent in the air was cleansing, and Miranda felt her shoulders become looser. A snapping of twigs behind her made her quicken her pace until a voice called, "Wait for us."

The two of them turned. It was Z19, the boy who had spoken so eloquently in the minibus after leaving Zephyr. His name was Joel. Coming up behind him was Z91 Febcon, Bella. Miranda was overjoyed to see them. The four of them fell into step and ploughed on through the undergrowth.

Abruptly, the woodland opened to an escarpment, vast sheets of rock pushing up out of the ground to create a barrier to their escape.

"Which way?" asked Joel.

"Over here," Bella beckoned to them and pointed to a narrow, overgrown track leading steeply up the side of the rock face.

The four of them scrambled up, briars catching their faces and hands; nettles stinging and branches whipping back as they climbed. Miranda wondered what they were going to do. This was crazy! Where could they go? She lifted her leg high to step over a protruding tree root and gasped as something dug into her flesh. Pulling herself up, she took a moment to rest and felt inside her pocket. Breathing hard, she pulled out the plastic card Patrick had given her for the phone.

"Frankie! I know what we can do!" she called to his retreating back. He paused and turned moving a foot to one side to balance, but the rock he had chosen was loose, and he began to slither down the hill, his shout echoing against the rockface.

"Quick, grab him, Joel!" Miranda shouted.

Joel had mercifully found a ledge to stand upon, and he caught Frankie by the arm, they both nearly went flying except for a tree trunk, preventing them going any further.

"Thanks," Frankie said, patting himself down and rubbing off some of the mud covering his clothes.

"I'm at the top. Keep to your left." A shout from Bella, higher up on the ridge gave them the confidence to keep moving.

Soon, they all stood surveying the scene. They were at the top of this section of the hillside and could see far down beyond into the valley where a road snaked up through the green fields and there, down a short lane, sat the old garage, with a red sports car and a black van parked on the forecourt. "I knew it!" she gasped. From their vantage point, they observed the doors of the garage opening and the two vehicles starting up, before disappearing into the cavernous space.

Miranda stared up at the long hill rising from the flat countryside surrounding it and dominating the landscape and then cast her eyes back towards the garage. "That's another of the schools. It must be hidden under the hill."

"I think you're right," Frankie agreed. The doors of the garage closed, leaving the rusty old trucks, parked outside, to fend for themselves.

"What was your idea?" he asked, suddenly grimacing.

"You okay?" Bella asked.

"Yes. No, not really. I twisted my ankle in that fall." Frankie dropped to the ground and started to rub his lower leg. "Miranda?" he urged again.

"I still have Patrick's card." Miranda once more pulled the card out of her jeans' pocket. A miniature paper boat sailed out, and Bella caught it before it crashed against the rocks below. "Oh, and we have Mal's number. It's on there," she said, pointing to the paper boat.

Joel spoke quietly. "Miranda," he said. "We knew you would save us. You helped to bring us here. You helped us find our identity, our names. You started it all."

She was confused. "It wasn't me – it was Frankie who brought us all together. He began the Teardrops, not me."

"He found one of your paper boats and read of the sorrow and anguish you were feeling, the many tears you had shed. It made him cry," Joel explained, rubbing at the tight black curls pushing through his scalp. "You were the catalyst that began a chain reaction. Knowing others were unhappy just as he was, led Frankie to find out more through his computing skills. Yes, he has brought us together, but you and your paper boats have set us free on an unknown ocean created by our own tears."

Silently, the four of them raised their hands high, making the teardrop shape; bringing their hands to touch they created butterflies. "Trefoil must not win. Together we will fight and be true to one another," Miranda said.

"True Tears!" they all shouted together.

Erin and Petra skirted round the house, crouching down whenever they saw one of the men stationed in the grounds. They finally arrived at the building, housing the swimming pool. Opening the door, the sweet sickly smell of chlorine invaded Erin's nostrils, and a gentle humming came from deep within the darkness.

"It's okay, it's only me," whispered Petra, switching on one of the main ceiling lights. Two figures emerged from the shadows – one was Cassie, Petra's twin, and the other a boy, whose white-blond stubble and pale features gave him the look of a ghost.

"This is Z37 – Dominic," explained Cassie gesturing towards the boy. He nodded to Erin. "It's good to see you. Have you any news about Bianca and Neal?"

Erin shrugged. "I don't know what happened to them or Shay. I'm so sorry. Cara attacked my Dad; I had to leave him there." She stifled a sob and then with defiance she lifted her head high. "I shall never forgive her for everything she's done to my family."

"We need to hide," said Petra. "Follow me." They all crept past the smooth, still water to a green door. While Petra unlocked the padlock and removed the chain, Erin stood gazing around her. Huge artificial palm trees stood guard at the side of the oval-shaped pool; wooden reclining sunbeds with cream coloured cushions were dotted around on the tiled floor; potted plants lazily trailed their long leaves into the pool. It all looks remarkably normal, Erin thought.

A tiny movement in the water caught her eye, and she ran to the edge. A sunny-yellow butterfly was desperately trying to flap its wings against the pull of the water. Putting the rolled-up road atlas down as she knelt, she scooped up the exhausted insect and, with her hands cupped to protect it, Erin laid the butterfly onto the leaves of a nearby plant. "You're free now, little one."

The humming sound intensified as they entered what was clearly the engine room. A dry warmth enveloped them, welcoming them into a space with pipes of all widths and lengths protruding from the far wall. Dials glowed indicating temperature and levels of chemicals, while rows of buttons and handles waited to be pushed and pulled. Erin turned to see Petra looping the chain and clicking the padlock closed on the outside door handle. She then flicked the latch and pulled the door shut.

"How did you learn to do that?" Erin asked, pushing a mass of coiled tubes out of the way to give them all more space.

"I watch a lot of murder mysteries," grinned Petra as she flipped a switch extinguishing all the lights.

They were just in time. The bang of a door crashing against a wall echoed through the building.

"Where's the light switch for this place?" came a throaty growl.

A gravelly voice exclaimed, "Bloomin' rich people 'aving a swimming pool. Very la-di-da!" It was apparent, to the four hidden away, the men were blundering about in the dark. Erin detected sounds of furniture being scraped along the floor and the two men swearing loudly.

"Oh, no! The map! It's still out there!" exclaimed Erin. Petra opened the door carefully, so as not to dislodge the chain. Dominic crawled out into the darkness and then laying himself flat on the floor, he reached out to grab the atlas. He slid back in, and Petra closed the door just as the main pool lights were clicked on. They all stood against the door to prevent anyone entering their little cell.

"Let's check down 'ere. I heard summat," the gravelly voice said. The tramp of feet came closer until Erin sensed someone was directly outside. The chain rattled, boot-clad feet kicked the wood. The four held their posts.

"They won't be in there. Look it's locked from the outside." This was a woman's voice. Erin held her breath as she recognised the dulcet tones of Cara. She tightened her hands into fists.

"I could get some bolt cutters, Miss Mallory."

"Come on; you're wasting time. Even they can't magic themselves into a locked room, you idiot! We must get back to Terra school. We've lost a few of the brats, but don't worry; we'll get them. They won't have gone far." The voices and footsteps trailed away.

The four young people hidden away in their warm cocoon, let out sighs of relief. Waiting until they thought they were alone and safe, they finally relaxed and slumped down to sit with their backs against the door, their legs out in front of them. Erin rested her head on Petra's shoulder and dozed.

A loud bang outside jolted Erin awake. Sounds like someone's letting off fireworks, she thought in the bleary state between sleep and wakefulness. An explosive boom made her scramble to her feet and click on the lights, causing them all to blink and rub their eyes. The others also clambered to their feet, and Petra pushed the door open; the chain falling to the floor with a clang. An orange light seeped through the windows. Erin ran towards the entrance and tugged the door open. Night had fallen; the moon stealing away the August sunshine to keep it hidden for another day. A strange reddish-orange glow lit up the house. Thick grey clouds seemed to cling to the bricks before billowing out into the night. The air was rank with smoke. The house was on fire!

Erin screamed and Petra, Cassie and Dominic dashed to the door. Petra shouted, "Mum... Dad!" and ran towards the blazing building.

"No, Petra! Come back!" Erin yelled, hastening after her friend. Reaching the patio, where only the day before she had shown Patrick the tablet, Erin caught up with Petra. The fierce heat held them back and rooted them to the spot. Suddenly, the glass doors of the games room exploded outwards; tongues of orange and red flames licking at the cool air.

"It's no good," Dominic shouted from behind them. "We have to make a run for it. I have the map. Let's go!"

Petra clung to Erin. "What if they're still in there?"

"Dominic's right, we have to get away from here. If they can do this, then they might kill us too!" Cassie shouted above the crackling roar of the beast threatening to consume the whole building. Bright cinders were spiralling their way up plumes of black smoke.

They crept silent as the dead from their viewing area across dry, spiky grass to the edge of the garden where a wooden stile took them over the fence into a broad field. Smoke filled the air and tears filled their eyes. The glow from the fire lit their way as they stumbled and staggered through neat rows of wheat. Arriving at a gate into another field, they wearily climbed over the bars. The dark of the night was now suffocating, the light of the fire far behind them. A few more fields finally brought them to a road.

Petra whirled round to Erin. "What now? Where do we go? Who can help us?"

Dominic spoke quietly. "Erin," he said. "The Teardrops knew you would be our saviour. You helped us find our identity, our names. You gave us a taste of the outside world."

She was confused. "It was Frankie who brought us all together. He began the Teardrops, not me."

Cassie murmured, "You saved us from that hellhole. We know you will save us."

Petra nodded. "You brought my sister to me, Erin."

Erin stared back at them. All three were waiting for her to speak, to make decisions. She lifted her head. "Okay," she said. "What do we have? We have a map, and I have a memory stick."

"I have a bit of money," announced Petra, holding up a couple of ten-pound notes from her pocket.

"We need to plan where to go and what to do," Erin said. "We'll have to find somewhere until the morning. That'll do," she said, pointing to a stone-built bus shelter perched next to the road. The four of them tumbled in. A wooden ledge allowed Cassie and Petra to sit while Erin and Dominic tried to make themselves comfortable on the cold, dusty ground.

Leaning against the stone wall of the shelter, Dominic said sadly, "We can't fight against Trefoil. We need an army, not a battalion."

Erin smiled. "Then we must adopt different methods to close the four schools down, to discover what Trefoil's real plans are and bring them to justice."

Silently, the four of them raised their hands high making the teardrop shape; bringing their hands to touch they created butterflies. "Trefoil must not win. Together we will fight and be true to one another," Erin said.

"True Tears!" they all shouted together.

TO BE CONTINUED ...

True Tears

ACKNOWLEDGEMENTS

First of all, I must give an enormous thank you to all my readers, both young and young at heart. Your wonderful comments following book one, Paper Boats and Butterflies: Unfolding the Truth, mean so much and give me a warm, fuzzy feeling in my heart. This keeps me going, especially during those times I doubt myself and my writing. It is so lovely that you like my characters as much as I do, and I hope you have enjoyed their continuing story in True Tears.

Huge thanks and much love go to my family and friends who have supported me with my first book and now the second in the trilogy. Thank you for reading book one, for telling me to keep going, for making me gallons of tea, for your lovely comments on social media, for reminding me I am now an author and to be proud of what I have achieved.